ENCHANTED

A novel based on the Walt Disney Pictures movie
Adapted by Jasmine Jones
Based on the screenplay written by Bill Kelly
Executive Producers Chris Chase, Sunil Perkash, Ezra Swerdlow
Produced by Barry Josephson and Barry Sonnenfeld
Directed by Kevin Lima

DISNEY PRESS
New York

Copyright © 2007 Disney Enterprises, Inc.

All rights reserved. Published by Disney Press, an imprint of Disney Book Group.
No part of this book may be reproduced or transmitted in any form or by any
means, electronic or mechanical, including photocopying,
recording, or by any information storage and retrieval system, without
written permission from the publisher. For information address
Disney Press, 114 Fifth Avenue, New York, New York 10011-5690.

Printed in the United States of America

First Edition
1 3 5 7 9 10 8 6 4 2

Library of Congress Catalog Card Number: 2007901737

ISBN-13: 978-1-4231-0471-1
ISBN-10: 1-4231-0471-4
For more Disney Press fun, visit www.disneybooks.com
Visit EnchantedMovie.com

Chapter One

Once upon a time, in a magical kingdom known as Andalasia, there lived an evil queen named Narissa. Selfish and cruel, she lived in fear that one day her stepson, Edward, would marry, and she would lose her throne forever. And so she did all in her power to prevent the prince from ever meeting the one special maiden with whom he would share true love's kiss.

Deep in the woods of Andalasia, there lived a beautiful young maiden named Giselle. Pure of heart and bright of spirit, she enchanted all who knew her. While there were not many people so deep in the woods, Giselle was never alone. She had plenty of animal friends to keep her company. And like anyone who met Giselle, the animals loved her dearly. So, Giselle spent her days singing and dancing, with no reason to ever be sad or angry. It was the perfect life for a perfect maiden. . . .

Now, on this particular day, Giselle was busy making a statue out of twigs, bark, and leaves, while humming a lovely little tune.

"Giselle!" Two bluebirds flew through her open window, chirping happily. "Giselle! How about this for your statue?"

Giselle smiled sweetly, tossing her long red hair over her shoulder. "Oh!" she cried. "This will be perfect! Thank you!" She placed the acorn at the exact center of the statue's face.

"Okay, you mokes, move it!" bellowed Giselle's best friend, Pip. Pip was a rather small, rather loud, chipmunk. While he was not the largest of the woodland creatures, his heart was big for his size, and he loved nothing more than helping Giselle. "We've got a face to put together here, while it's still ingrained in her subcranium!"

"Oh, Pip, it was such a lovely dream," Giselle said, sighing happily. "We were holding hands and dancing and . . ."

A bunny hopped over and placed two glittering stones in her palm. "These for the eyes?"

"Blue!" Giselle beamed at the bunny, giving him an affectionate pat on the head. "Oh, how did you know? And they sparkle, just like his!" She stood back to see how they looked. "Yes, that's it!"

Pip clapped his tiny paws. "Okay, everybody!" he hollered to the forest animals gathered in Giselle's living room. "The moment we've all been waiting for." He motioned to Giselle. "Floor's yours, honey."

"Presenting my one true love . . ." Giselle turned the statue to face the row of excited animals. "My prince! My dream come true!"

Pip stood back to get a good look at the statue and held back a groan. Art this was not. A bird's nest made up the "prince's" hair; nuts for his ears; and a body made of twigs. Pip paused before admitting: "If that's your dream, you might wanna think about goin' back to bed."

"Oh, my goodness!" Giselle's blue eyes widened in alarm.

"What? What's the problem?" Pip asked.

"I didn't give him any lips!" Giselle cried.

"Does he have to have lips?" a fawn asked.

Giselle smiled at the young deer. "Of course!" Without lips, the man of her dreams could not bestow the most important gift of love—true love's kiss. Giselle knew that true love's kiss was more powerful than anything in the whole world. Turning to the rest of her friends she added, "If we're going to find a perfect pair of lips, we're going to need a lot more help!"

So, as Giselle began to sing about true love, the creatures got to work. Giselle needed her kiss!

Deep in the forest, Prince Edward's dark hair whipped in the wind. He gave a yank on the lasso in his hand, pulling it tighter around the troll beneath him. "Look out below!" Edward called as the troll fell to the ground with a mighty crash. Seeing the immobilized creature, Edward puffed up his chest. He truly was a great slayer of beasts. A hero, really.

"Amazing, sire!" Edward's valet, Nathaniel, apparently agreed. Carefully, Nathaniel picked his way around the troll. "Your tenth troll this month!" The portly man tried to climb the enormous beast's face, but slipped on its lip, accidentally shoving his hand into the troll's left nostril. Nathaniel grimaced. While it was his duty to encourage Edward's troll hunting, he wished it weren't quite so . . . slimy. Looking down at the captive, he forced a polite smile. "Oh, I love hunting trolls!" Nathaniel exclaimed, hoping he sounded believable. "Big trolls! Little trolls! Trolls, trolls, trolls!"

As Edward looked down at the creature, some of the excitement in his blue eyes dimmed. Lately, the thrill of troll-hunting just hadn't been the same. It felt as though something was missing. "Trolls are fine to pass the time, Nathaniel," the prince said with a sigh. "But my heart longs to be joined in song."

Suddenly, a lovely voice filled the air. It was far away, but as clear as fresh water from a bubbling stream.

Prince Edward stood stock-still. "Do you hear that, Nathaniel?" he cried.

Nathaniel gulped. "Me? No," he said quickly. "I hear nothing. Nothing at all, Your Highness."

But Edward wasn't listening.

"I must find the maiden that belongs to that sweet voice!" With a mighty leap, Prince Edward bounded into the saddle. His pure white steed set off at a gallop the moment he cried, "Ride, Destiny!" The horse and rider quickly plunged into the forest at top speed in pursuit of the enchanting voice.

"Oh, poo!" Nathaniel sighed. "This isn't good. All these years of troll chasing, trying to keep him from ever meeting a girl. Oh, the queen, she's not going to like this!" He pictured Edward's stepmother, Queen Narissa—so beautiful . . . so vicious. She had been sending Edward—and therefore Nathaniel—on more and more troll hunts lately. She wanted to keep the handsome young man as far away from potential wives as possible. And so far, it had worked. But now this!

What will I do? Nathaniel wondered, frantic at the thought of the prince chasing after a lovely singing voice, which was most likely coming from a rather lovely lass. The queen specifically told me to keep him away from any possibility of true love. . . .

Just then, a groan broke into Nathaniel's thoughts. The troll was waking up!

Nathaniel smiled. He'd just had a brilliant idea. Quickly, he pulled a dagger from his belt and cut the troll's bonds. In a flash, the troll had taken off after the prince, leaving a pleased Nathaniel behind.

Meanwhile, Prince Edward and Destiny galloped through the woods, growing closer to the voice.

Just then, the troll leaped over Prince Edward's head, startling the handsome man. The troll quickly darted ahead, outpacing Destiny's gallop. Prince Edward was the least of the troll's worries now. He was on his way to capture the owner of the delicate voice. Whoever she was, the troll felt sure that she would make a tasty snack.

"You shall not prevail, foul troll!" Prince Edward called. "That maiden is mine!"

But the troll had already disappeared.

Chapter Two

"Honey, do you really think your 'dream boy' exists?" Pip asked, as Giselle sat gazing through her window, a dreamy expression on her face and her song over.

"Oh, Pip." Sighing, Giselle turned to face her friend. "I know he's out there somewhere."

Unfortunately, at that moment, someone very *undreamy* arrived. An enormous, ugly eye appeared at the window. With her back turned, Giselle didn't see it.

"Eye! Eye! Eye . . ." the forest animals stammered.

"I . . . I . . . I what?" Giselle asked.

"I eat you now!" the troll answered as his thick arm smashed through the window.

Crash! With a scream, Giselle backed away from the window.

"Everybody scatter!" Pip ordered. The woodland creatures obeyed as the troll's other huge hand plunged through the roof. "Gotcha!" he cried, his hand closing around something solid.

But he didn't have Giselle. She had slipped through his fingers and hurried onto the roof. She leaped into the branches of a nearby tree.

"Huh?" The troll blinked. Pulling his arm out of the cottage, the troll saw that he was holding Giselle's prince statue. "Hey! That's cheating!" he said. "I supposed to eat you."

Thank goodness trolls aren't very smart, Giselle thought as she climbed higher, higher . . .

But the troll came after her. He soon reached her branch.

"Oh, no, ya don't, ya big lug!" Pip shouted from the branches above. With the speed of a cannonball,

Pip launched himself down at the troll's head. It made a hollow coconut sound.

All three were now on one branch.

Creak! The branch began to bend.

"Yikes," Pip muttered to himself, "I gotta lay off all the nuts."

Giselle tightened her grip on the branch, but she was slipping. It was tottering under all the weight. . . .

"Girl yummy." The troll laughed gleefully.

Thwack!

"Hey!" The troll frowned. A princely sword had just pinned his sleeve to the tree limb.

Giselle barely had time to wonder where the sword came from, because in the next moment, she saw him—her vision. The prince of her dreams. He was riding toward her on a white horse. . . .

"Fear not, fair maiden, I am here!" Edward called up to Giselle.

The sound of her dream man's voice snapped Giselle back to reality—a reality in which she was now sliding off the end of a bough, head over feet. She was about to fall a very long way. . . .

"Gotcha!" Pip cried as he raced to the end of the branch, grabbing Giselle's toe. For a moment, he stopped her slide.

Pip breathed a sigh of relief . . .

. . . until Giselle started sliding again! She was too heavy for him! After all, while Pip was strong of heart, he was still a chipmunk. As he watched, Giselle fell off the end of the branch and onto the bough below.

"Uh-oh," the troll said—just before the now lighter branch snapped back, shooting him high into the air and far away.

While the troll was no longer a threat, Giselle now had another problem. She was slipping off a branch . . . again! Panicked, Giselle called up to her friend. "Pip!"

Four of her fingers still clung to the branch, then three, then two . . .

"Hang on!" Pip cried, "Hang on, honey!" Pip lunged at her thumb, but it was too late.

Giselle screamed as she fell down through the branches . . .

. . . into the very strong, waiting arms of Prince Edward.

"Oh, my gosh!" Giselle said breathlessly, for the prince's blue eyes were sparkling into her own. They were just like the polished stones in her bird's nest prince statue. Her heart hammered in her chest. "It's you!"

"Yes, it's me." Prince Edward smiled. "And you are?"

"Giselle."

"Giselle! We shall be married in the morning!" the prince announced.

There was no doubt about it—Prince Edward and Giselle had found true love.

But not everyone was happy with the beautiful scene. From deep in the castle, a tall, gorgeous queen stared into her crystal ball, watching the joyful moment.

It was Narissa—and she was *very* angry. She had tried so hard, for so long, to keep this very thing from happening. After all, if Edward were to marry, she would no longer be queen. That was why she put up with Nathaniel's simpering and the ever-present threat of trolls. It meant Edward stayed busy.

"Oh, so this is the little forest rat who thinks she can steal my throne," she said in a sugary voice. Then, her rage boiled over and she smashed the ball to clear the picture of Edward and Giselle. She let out a hideous cry—"NEVER!"

There was one thing, she, Queen Narissa, was sure of. Edward may have found his true love. But he would never marry Giselle. Never.

Not if there was anything she could do about it.

Chapter
Three

Giselle was so excited when she pulled up to the castle the next morning that she opened her carriage door rather quickly. "Oh, excuse me!" she cried, realizing that she had just smashed Nathaniel in the face with the door. "I am so sorry! Am I late? I do hope I'm not late!" She hopped out in a rush of white.

Nathaniel shook his head and tried to smile, his handkerchief pressed against his nose. "No, miss. Just in time!"

"Oh, thank goodness!"

Nathaniel was just about to shut the door to the carriage when Pip popped out.

"Honey, wait up!" Pip called. "We ain't done with you yet!"

Animals poured out of the carriage, knocking Nathaniel over in the process. They took no notice of the valet—they were too busy hurrying after Giselle. Two bunnies wrapped a ribbon around her waist, and a pair of bluebirds flew a diamond tiara into her shining hair.

"Thank you!" Giselle told her friends.

"You're welcome, Giselle!" the bluebirds trilled.

In a billow of white, Giselle swept through the castle doors, Nathaniel right on her heels. Turning, he bowed courteously to the animals—and then shut the door in their faces.

"And what do we look like?" Pip cried, furiously. "Garbage?" The other animals stood before the door, forlorn and unsure of what to do. But the chipmunk bounded away, determined to find another way in.

As far as Pip was concerned, this wasn't over.

* * *

"Oh," Giselle said as Nathaniel led her through the royal courtyard, "to think that in just a few moments . . . that Edward and I . . . that he and me . . . Oh, that we . . . Oh, my!"

This last "oh, my" was because an old hag had just stepped in front of Giselle.

"Hello, my dear," the hag said in a creaky voice. "What a lovely bride."

"That's very kind of you," Giselle said uncertainly. She tried to step around the old woman, but the crone blocked her path.

"Old granny has a wedding gift for you, child."

Giselle cleared her throat. She was fairly certain that she didn't want whatever the old woman had to offer. Still, she didn't want to be rude. "Thank you. But I really should be going . . . . You see . . ."

"'Tis a wishing well, dear!" the hag broke in. Grabbing Giselle's arm, the crone dragged her toward a beautiful waterfall pouring into an old well.

"But all my wishes are about to come true!" Giselle protested as the hag pushed her toward the well. "Excuse me, I really do have to go. . . ."

"But a wish on your wedding day!" the old woman insisted, her eyes gleaming wickedly. "That's the most magical of all. Just close your eyes, my darling, and make your wish. That's right. Lean in close. Are you wishing for something?"

Giselle's chest felt heavy, almost as though the well itself was trying to pull her in. "Yes, I am." Smiling, she closed her eyes and began to whisper, "And they both lived happily ever af—"

But before Giselle could finish her wish, the hag pushed her in!

Giselle's scream echoed all the way down the well. It didn't stop. It simply seemed to fade away, as if her voice had disappeared into another dimension.

Back in the courtyard, the hag laughed quietly to herself. The perfect crime, she thought. With no witnesses.

But she was wrong. There was one witness. For Pip had found his own way into the royal courtyard. He had seen the whole thing. Watching his dear Giselle fall into the well, his mind froze for a moment, and the chipmunk couldn't think what to do. Then it occurred to him. "Help!" he said at last. "Edward! Prince Edward, we need help!" Quickly, he bounded away in search of the prince. Unfortunately, that meant he did not see what happened next.

"*Speciosus, formosus, praeclarus . . .*" the hag chanted. Suddenly, her face melted and shifted. One moment she was an old woman, and the next—the beautiful Queen Narissa!

"Where?" asked a voice from the shadows. A moment later, Nathaniel appeared. He looked very confused and frightened. "Where my most adored queen? Where did you send her?" He peered into the well.

The queen smiled cruelly. "To a place where there are no 'happily ever afters'!" she cackled.

It was a long way down. Giselle twirled and tumbled down the well, and as she tumbled, she noticed something strange. Sparkly dust was floating every-where. It landed all over her, and in a moment, her skin began changing. Her dress was changing, too. It was as if she were expanding—going from two dimensions to three. Above her, silver dust swirled into the shape of a dancing couple.

Thump!

Giselle landed hard in a very dark space. The sparkling dust was gone. All around her was quiet, except for the drip, drip, drip of water. "Oh my!" Giselle said. She had a suspicion she was far away from Andalasia.

Giselle looked around, fear edging into her usually cheerful demeanor. On the ground in front of her, five small holes shot shafts of light through the darkness. At last—a way out! She climbed toward the holes and peered through. It was some sort of cover. Giselle moved the heavy metal aside and pushed herself through the round hole—into the unknown.

Chapter Four

"Oh, my goodness!" Giselle said with a gasp. She was in a strange place filled with wonders she had never seen or even imagined. Enormous buildings towered overhead. Boxes with moving images flashed from boards posted high above, and bright lights beamed all around her. Yellow vehicles that moved without horses whizzed past. And there were people *everywhere!*

Giselle was in the center of Times Square in New York City—a busy, bustling place, full of tourists, theme shops, and theaters. Giselle grunted as she tried to pull herself through the manhole. The wide skirt of her puffy white wedding dress strained against the hole, until finally—*poof!*—it squeezed its way out, snapping back into its original shape.

Giselle stood up.

Honk!

Four cars slammed down on their brakes to avoid hitting her—and ended up crashing in a perfect square. In her huge white dress, Giselle looked like the marshmallow at the center of their graham cracker.

All the drivers got out of their cars and began to shout and point. They seemed to be yelling at each other, so she just picked up her skirts and scurried onto the sidewalk.

"Hello!" Giselle shouted as a crowd of people streamed around her. "Excuse me! Pardon me! I wonder if one of you kind people might direct me to the castle?" The crowd hurried past. No one even glanced in her direction. But Giselle didn't give up. True, they looked unlike anyone or anything she'd seen in Andalasia, but that didn't mean they couldn't help. "Please! If you could just point me toward the castle?"

Giselle stumbled as she bumped into someone.

"Hey!" protested a voice from somewhere between the folds of her skirts. "Watch it, will ya?"

Giselle gathered her white hem and stared down at a small man in a severe suit. He scowled up at her with a familiar expression, and—for a moment— she thought she recognized him. "Grumpy?" she cried.

"Geez lady, are you for real?" With a growl, the small man stormed away.

Well, Giselle thought, he certainly was grumpy— even if that wasn't his name!

She stepped backward, and found herself swept into a wave of human traffic. Soon, she found herself underground again—in the middle of the gritty New York City subway. "Excuse me!" Giselle called as the businesspeople eager to get home from work pushed her down the stairs. "I'm supposed to be at the ball to wed my one true love, Prince . . . Edward! Edward?"

* * *

A while later, Giselle emerged from the subway in a completely different neighborhood. The street was littered with garbage. Ugly shops lined the curbs. Giselle felt as dingy as the street itself—her once pristine white dress was streaked with dirt, and the elaborate hairdo her furry friends had fashioned for the wedding was about to tumble. Her feet were aching. At last, she decided that she could go no further. She sat down on a stoop next to an old man who was staring at her as if she were a creature from another planet. Which, in a way, she was.

"Hello, old man," Giselle said gently. "May I sit with you? I'm very tired, and I'm scared. I've never been this far from home, and I'm not sure at all where I am. If someone could show me just a bit of kindness, a friendly hello, or even a smile, I think that would lift my spirits so much."

Slowly, the filthy old man opened his mouth in a wide, snaggly, rotted grin. Giselle gulped hard. That smile was hardly the encouragement she had been looking for.

"Oh . . . you have a lovely smile," she lied.

Suddenly—with more speed than Giselle could have imagined—the old man plucked the diamond tiara from her hair and ran away!

"Oh, my gosh!" Giselle cried as her long red hair tumbled into her face. "Come back!" she shouted, hurrying after him. "Please!" But the man turned a corner and disappeared from sight. "You are not a very nice old man!" she called.

Just then, the skies opened up, and heavy rain began to fall, soaking her to the skin.

Giselle had always wanted to have an adventure, but this one wasn't going well at all.

Then, off in the distance, she saw a sign. It was an actual sign—a billboard that read, THE PALACE CASINO, ATLANTIC CITY—WHERE DREAMS COME TRUE. Above the words was a glorious pink castle. Her castle, she was sure of it.

Giselle smiled, her blue eyes twinkling. For the first time that day, she knew where she was going.

Across town in one of New York's most prominent

law firms, a handsome young divorce attorney named Robert Phillip was trapped in his office. His eyes drifted lazily from one side of the table to the other, watching disinterestedly as a couple negotiated the terms of their divorce. Or rather, screamed their demands into one another's faces.

"No!" shrieked Mrs. Phoebe Banks. "No way you're getting Hank!"

"You just want him because I want him!" Mr. Ethan Banks barked.

Unable to find anything in his paperwork, Mr. Banks's lawyer looked up. "Wait a minute," he said, momentarily breaking the argument. "Excuse me, guys. I'm getting confused here. Who's Hank?"

The couple turned simultaneously to look at him; Ethan looked as though his lawyer had just said the most ridiculous thing he'd ever heard. "Hank Aaron," he informed him. "Milwaukee Braves! His 1954 rookie card!"

Robert raised his eyebrows, unable to believe how absurd this had become. "A baseball card? That's what this gets down to is a baseball card?"

Robert let out a weary sigh just as his assistant, Sam, entered the office and nodded at him. "It's time."

Robert immediately rose to his feet, gathering all his papers into a stack to be put into his briefcase. "Excuse me." He turned to address his client. "I have to pick up my daughter."

Robert was off to tell his daughter that he wanted to ask Nancy, his girlfriend, to marry him. Robert thought his relationship with Nancy was smart and practical. Just the way he liked it.

Chapter Five

"How'd it go tonight?" Robert asked his daughter, Morgan, as he buttoned her raincoat. Morgan's karate class had just let out, and the rest of the students were streaming onto the sidewalk behind her.

"Dad, nobody's socializing, like you said," Morgan complained. "It's just kicking and hitting each other."

"Sweetie, that's kind of what they do in karate," Robert said as he tried to hail a cab.

Morgan looked up at him. "You said if I didn't like it—"

Robert sighed and ran a hand through his thick, dark hair. His dark eyes looked tired, and he tried to keep from frowning. "I know," he said. "Why don't we just see how it goes? Sometimes it takes a little time, you know?"

"I guess." Morgan shrugged. She didn't like karate, but she *hated* disappointing her father.

"Good-bye, Morgan." One of her classmates approached with a big smile.

Morgan hid shyly behind her dad.

"Morgan, sweetie," Robert urged, "say good-bye."

The six year old managed a shy wave as her father opened the door to the yellow cab that had finally stopped.

"One hundred sixteenth and Riverside," Robert told the driver as he and Morgan slid into the back-seat. He buckled Morgan's seat belt as the cab took off. "Since you were so good about karate, I bought you a little something." He pulled a gift-wrapped package from his briefcase and placed it on her lap.

Morgan grinned. "For me?"

"Uh-huh. Now I've got to warn you," Robert said

as Morgan happily ripped off the paper, "it's not that fairy-tale book you've wanted . . . but I do think you're really going to like . . ."

Morgan tore away the rest of the wrapping paper and held up the gift. "A book?"

This wasn't just any book. This wasn't a fairy tale, like the one you're reading now, or an adventure, or a funny story about someone like Morgan herself. No, this was a book entitled, *Important Women of Our Time.*

It sounded very dreary to Morgan. Still, she was polite, and she tried her best to seem excited about the gift. "Thanks," she said softly.

"It's about famous women from the twentieth century, you know?" Robert said in a rush, aware of his daughter's disappointment. "Smart, successful women struggling to do really great things." He sighed. The woman at the bookstore had told him that any little girl would love a book like this one. Clearly, she had been wrong.

Morgan looked out the window. "Uh-huh."

"Look at this." Robert took the book from her

hands and pointed to a photograph. "See? Rosa Parks. Here's Marie Curie. She was a remarkable woman who dedicated her life to research. . . ." He cleared his throat. "Until she died from radiation poisoning."

"She died?" Morgan blinked at him.

"Yes, well," Robert admitted. "It was in the name of science." Just then his BlackBerry chirped, saving him from any further explanation. Robert picked it up quickly. "Hello? Hi, hon. What? Tomorrow morning's great. About seven-thirty?" He smiled over at his daughter. "Yeah, I'm with Morgan right now. Okay. Bye." Hanging up, he explained, "That was Nancy."

"Uh-huh." Morgan turned back to the window.

"She's really busy at work," Robert said. "She's got a lot going on. Having her own design studio. All that fashion stuff. She's like the women in this book. Someone to look up to. Someone *you* could look up to." He put his arm around Morgan's shoulder. "Sweetie," Robert said, "I'm going to ask her to marry me."

Morgan snapped to attention. "What?"

"You like her, right?"

Morgan thought for a moment. "She's good."

"I mean, we all get along," Robert said. "We have fun, don't you think?"

"Where's she going to live?" Morgan asked.

"Well . . . with us."

Morgan looked worried. "Do I have to give up my bedroom?"

"No. You don't have to give up your bedroom. No. Come on, it's going to be great! I promise." Robert squeezed Morgan's shoulder. "It's not like she's going to try and be your mother."

Morgan's eyes narrowed. "You mean *step*mother."

"Right. She's gonna be a *nice* stepmother," Robert corrected. "She even wants to take you to school tomorrow. Just you and her. For some 'grown-up girl' bonding time."

"I'm only six."

Robert smiled, revealing perfectly white, gleaming teeth. "You won't always be."

The taxi stopped at a red light, and Morgan turned back to the window. "Daddy, why is there a princess on the castle billboard?"

It was not an odd question. Because right outside, high above the cab, Giselle was beating on the billboard, begging to be let into the castle. She had managed to climb the ladder to the sign, and she wasn't about to leave until she got into the palace.

But Robert was busy scrolling through his e-mail on his BlackBerry and was oblivious to the rather strange scene. "It's an advertisement. It's a mannequin."

Morgan, however, was determined to find out what was going on. In fact, she was so curious that she completely forgot to be shy. "She's really there!" Morgan shouted, opening the taxi door and leaving.

Morgan's shout finally got Robert's attention. "Wait! What are you doing?" He called after Morgan as he, too, bolted from the cab. Following his daughter's glance up, Robert spotted Giselle . . . who was at that very moment, slipping along the edge of the billboard.

"Sweetie, wait here!" Robert told his daughter, following her out onto the street. "Hey, you!" he called up to Giselle. "Lady!"

Giselle looked around, finally realizing that the

voices were not coming from the palace, but rather from below. "Oh. Hello!" She smiled weakly—and just then, her foot slipped on the edge of the sign. She plunged off the billboard, barely grabbing the edge of the catwalk with one hand. "Ahhhhhh!"

"Catch her, Daddy!"

"Oh, no!" Robert cried, running forward to help. "Wait . . . !"

But Giselle's fingers were slipping—and then, just as she had in Andalasia, she was falling. . . .

"Ow!" Giselle cried as she landed half in Robert's arms, and half on the pavement.

"Ow!" Robert shouted. In his attempt to catch Giselle, he had hurt his arm.

Morgan, however, was very *unhurt*. She ran to Giselle and helped her to her feet. "Are you okay?"

"I'm fine," Giselle said.

"Oh, good," Robert said sarcastically, grimacing in pain at his arm. "I'm glad *you're* okay!"

"What were you doing up there?" Morgan asked Giselle.

Giselle rubbed her bruises and smiled at Morgan.

Finally, someone who seemed to care! "I was looking for some help," Giselle explained. "You see I've been wandering very far and long tonight. And I'm afraid nobody's been very nice to me."

"Yeah, well . . ." Robert scoffed. "Welcome to New York."

"Thank you!" Giselle grinned. It was so nice to finally be welcomed by someone!

Robert shrugged. "You sure you're all right?" he asked Giselle suspiciously. "You need me to call someone for you?"

Giselle looked confused. "I don't think they'd hear you from here!"

Ka-boom!

Just then, thunder tore across the sky. Robert wanted to tell Giselle to have a nice life and be on his way, but Morgan was staring up at him with wide, hopeful eyes. Robert sighed. He didn't like the idea of bringing a strange woman home and letting her use the telephone . . . but he *hated* disappointing his daughter.

Chapter
Six

"Then," Giselle said, as she, Morgan, and Robert spilled out of the elevator in their building, "the old hag said I should look in the well and wish for my heart's desire, but I must have looked in so far that I fell. Down and down and down! And then I climbed out of the round hole and got very lost until I fell off the castle, and now here I am with you."

While outside, rain was pouring down and the air had grown chilly, inside, the apartment building was warm and inviting. As Robert walked toward their door, he noticed that despite her fall and wet dress, Giselle seemed, well . . . awfully happy.

"Is this a big habit of yours?" Robert asked as he led Giselle down the hall to his apartment. "Falling off stuff?"

"Well, usually someone catches me," Giselle shrugged. "But not to worry! I'm certain Edward's already searching for me. No doubt, by morning he'll come and rescue me from this strange land! Take me home, and the two of us can share in true love's kiss!"

Robert arched an eyebrow. He was a lawyer. He believed in logic and law—not fairy tales and magic. "True love's kiss?" he asked skeptically.

Giselle nodded solemnly. "It's the most powerful thing in the world."

It took all of Robert's strength not to roll his eyes, but he managed it. "Right."

But Giselle didn't notice his sarcasm. A thought had just struck her. "If I could just find a place to rest my head for the night," Giselle said.

"What sort of place?" Robert asked warily.

"Oh, I don't know," Giselle admitted. "Maybe a nearby meadow or a hollow tree?"

"A hollow tree?" Robert repeated. Wow, this woman is really out there, he thought. What was she going to do—head over to Central Park and set up camp in the Sheep Meadow? Unfortunately, her next comment was even odder.

"Or a house full of dwarfs," Giselle said with a smile. "I hear they're very hospitable."

"Like I said, all I can really do is let you in for a few minutes if you want to dry off, use the phone." He put his key into the lock and swung open the door. "We have our own bedtime to stick to."

Morgan stepped inside, and Giselle started to follow—but her dress got stuck. Again.

"What is it with this dress of yours?" Robert asked. It *was* quite a dress for evening wear—even in New York City.

"Do you like it?" Giselle asked as she tried to yank herself through the door frame. "I gathered the silk from my silkworm friends, and I spun it into thread on my spinning wheel. . . ."

Morgan grabbed Giselle's hands and gave her a helpful tug. "You made it all by yourself?"

Robert helped, too, pulling as hard as he could. The huge hoop skirt sure was stubborn!

"Well . . . not all of it," Giselle admitted. "The mice and rabbits did help with the sewing."

"They're good!" Morgan said brightly.

At that moment, Giselle popped through the door. Unfortunately, her hoop didn't. It stayed lodged in the frame while Giselle tumbled head over heels into the living room. She pulled her long skirt down from over her head and smiled up at Robert, completely unembarrassed.

"Why don't we see about getting you a car?" he suggested. He looked around for a phone book, but in the midst of the rather cluttered apartment, he couldn't see it. He wished he weren't such a terrible housekeeper.

"Couldn't she sleep here, Daddy?" Morgan asked, breaking into Robert's thoughts.

"Um," Robert said quickly. "No. That's a big *no*."

Giselle stretched out on the couch, yawning

hugely. Her adventure had completely exhausted her.

"Are you really a princess?" Morgan whispered to her.

"Not yet . . ." Giselle said softly. "But I will be . . . soon." And before she could say another word, Giselle fell asleep.

"Wow, Dad," Morgan said in amazement. "She is really sleepy."

Robert looked up from the phone book, which he had finally found under a pillow, to see Giselle fast asleep on his couch. "Oh, no!" he cried. "This is not acceptable."

"You're not really going to make her go, are you, Daddy?" Morgan pleaded.

Robert frowned. "I want you to go to bed, please!"

Morgan looked at the sleeping Giselle. "I think she might be a real princess."

"Morgan. Remember our talk?"

"But, Daddy . . ."

"Just because she has on a funny dress doesn't mean she's a princess!" Robert said. "She's a

seriously confused woman who's fallen in our laps!"
And she may need a mental-health specialist more
than our sympathy, he added silently.

Morgan thought that over. "So are we not gonna
let her stay?"

"Nope. Put on your nightgown and go to sleep.
Good night, okay?" He gave his daughter a hug and
watched as she padded off to her room. The moment
her door closed, he picked up the phone and
punched in a number.

"Town Car," said a man's voice.

"Hi," Robert said into the receiver. "I need a car at
one hundred sixteenth and Riverside."

But the dispatcher wasn't listening. "Can you
hold, please?" he asked. A split second later, Robert
found himself listening to the soft hold music. With
a sigh, he turned toward his window. Outside, heavy
rain pelted the glass. It was an ugly night.

Giselle stirred slightly on the couch and made a
small groan. Robert turned, and, for a moment, it felt
as though his heart might burst from his chest. The
lamp beside her head bathed her skin in a rosy glow,

and her hair seemed the color of a warm sunset. She looked beautiful, Robert thought with a pang. Morgan was right—she looked like a real princess.

All right, so maybe she was a little . . . off, Robert thought. But she didn't seem dangerous. Was there really any need to wake her up and send her out into the rain?

The music stopped, and the dispatcher came back on the line. "Hello, sir," he said. "Destination, please? Sir?"

Gently, Robert clicked off the phone and placed it on the side table. He had a horrible feeling that he was going to regret this decision—but he couldn't force Giselle out into the cold, wet night.

Back in Andalasia, Pip had finally managed to track down Prince Edward. Quickly, the chipmunk filled him in on Giselle, the hag, and the well. When he finally finished talking, Prince Edward leaped into action. His purple cloak flowing behind him and his eyes gleaming, he jumped into the well . . . and was immediately sucked into the vortex between worlds.

As he tumbled, head over feet, glittering dust began to shimmer around him.

"Fear not, Giselle! I will rescue you!" the prince called out.

Close behind him came Pip. He had no choice but to follow. Hearing Edward's cry, Pip sighed. "Who's gonna rescue me?"

Before Pip could say more, the dust disappeared, and with a thud, the odd pair landed on some very hard, and very *real*, ground.

In the middle of Times Square, three sewer workers stood around a manhole. It was the place where, only hours before, Giselle had suddenly emerged into the human world. They were about to place a new cover over the manhole when it began to hiss. In the next moment, a dashing prince shot through the manhole and landed, standing on the surrounding safety fence.

The sewer workers stared. "What in the . . . ?"

Prince Edward looked at the strange creatures before him. They're clearly peasants, he thought, but in what land have I arrived?

"Hey!" The supervisor—a meaty man named Arty—stepped forward to holler at the tights-wearing prince. "You ain't supposed to be down there! We got sewage mains, telecom circuits, fiber optics—"

In a flash, Prince Edward drew his sword. "Silence! Your name, peasant! Quickly!"

The supervisor gulped. "Arty."

"Are you in league with the wicked old hag who sent my poor Giselle to this foul place ... *Artee?*" The prince's lips twisted around the strange name.

Just then, with a whoosh, Pip shot through the manhole. Prince Edward plucked the chipmunk out of the air, as if he were an apple on a tree. He held Pip up to Arty's face. "Is this man party to this evil plot, chipmunk?"

"No," Pip said. Well, he didn't actually say that. Sure, he *tried* to. He moved his lips as he always had, but instead of a coherent explanation, only a chirp came out. Pip grabbed his throat. With a gasp, the chipmunk realized the horrible truth—he couldn't talk in this world!

Prince Edward smiled sympathetically. He had encountered this problem before. "Poor chipmunk. Speechless in my presence?" He turned back to Arty. "What say you, sir? Don't try my patience!"

"I don't even know what you're talking about!" Arty cried.

"I seek a beautiful girl," Edward said, his voice softening at the thought of Giselle. "A prince's delight. Her hair spun like the finest gold, her skin an alabaster white. My other half, my one coquette, the answer to my love's duet."

Arty cleared his throat uncomfortably. "I'd like to find one of them, too."

Edward narrowed his eyes. "Then keep a wary eye out, *Artee!*"

And with a nimble jump, his royal purple cape fluttering, Edward cleared the safety fence and dashed up the street. Pip hurried after him.

Arty and the other sewer workers stared after them. Then they shrugged. That was the thing about working in New York City—every day, you came across something weird.

Chapter
Seven

Giselle stretched sleepily, her eyes fluttering open. For a moment, she couldn't remember where she was. Then it came to her—the old hag, the well. She was in a strange land, staying with her new friends. But as she looked around she realized that her new friends were quite messy. Dirty clothes were strewn about, magazines had been dumped on the floor and abandoned, and the kitchen sink was full of dishes.

Giselle shook her head. "This just won't do!" she said, jumping up and straightening her rather disheveled white dress as best she could.

Robert and Morgan have been so kind in letting me stay with them, Giselle thought. The least I can do is tidy up.

And, of course, Giselle never tidied up without help. . . .

Putting her head through the open window, Giselle sang out in a clear, enchanting voice.

Across the city, wildlife sprang to attention. Unfortunately, the borough of Manhattan is a little short on bunnies, fawns, and bluebirds. It does, though, have furry animals. Well, okay, it has rats. But there are birds as well. Pigeons, to be exact.

The animals scurried and flapped to Robert's apartment. Rats poured in through the heating vents, pigeons fluttered in through the windows, and cockroaches streamed in through the pipes. Soon, a crowd of helpers waited eagerly for Giselle's instructions.

Giselle forced herself to smile. These . . . animals weren't exactly what she'd had in mind. Still, help was help. "Well, it's always nice to make new friends!" she said bravely. Then she clapped her hands three times. "All right, everyone! Let's tidy things up!"

The animals worked their hardest—the rats licked the dirty dishes clean, and the pigeons flapped the dust bunnies out the windows. The cockroaches worked as a team to carry out the garbage bags; then everyone headed to the bathroom. As they worked, Giselle continued to sing a happy tune. Even as she scrubbed the floor, she hummed and smiled.

Everyone was having so much fun cleaning that they didn't realize that they had woken Morgan. The young girl wandered into the hall just in time to see a group of rats tackling the laundry.

Morgan's eyes grew wide at the sight of rodents and bugs . . . cleaning. Letting out a squeak, she turned and ran down the hall. "Daddy!" Morgan ran into her father's room. "You have to come see!" she cried, shaking him awake. "Now!"

Robert sprang out of bed and dashed into the hallway. When he saw his apartment filled with vermin, his eyes went wide as well, but not in a good way. "What in the . . . ?" He charged into the living room, swatting at the rats and roaches. "Get out of here!" he shouted. He tiptoed carefully into the kitchen and grabbed a broom. "Morgan, quick!" he cried, nodding at the front door. "Open it!"

Morgan fought her urge to scream (after all, they were rats!) while she held the door open and Robert sent the pests scampering through it. Once they were safely outside, she slammed the door shut, shuddering.

The sudden silence in the apartment was broken by the sound of running water—and humming. Someone was singing in the shower! "Wait here!" Robert commanded.

Two pigeons were wrapping Giselle in a fluffy towel as Robert stormed into the bathroom. "Good morning, Robert!" Giselle chirped. "I hope you had nice dreams."

Robert blinked at the birds. "I think I'm still in one."

"This room is magic!" Giselle said, shaking her red hair dry. "Where does the water come from?"

Robert thought for a moment before answering. "Um . . . from the pipes."

"Where do the pipes get it?"

"I don't know," Robert said. "From . . . wherever the pipes get it."

Giselle smiled. "It *is* magical."

At that moment, the front doorbell rang, and Morgan hurried to answer it. It was Robert's girl-friend, Nancy. As usual, she was dressed beautifully, her dark wavy hair falling past her shoulders, a BlackBerry against her ear. She had a very successful clothing business—it was her job to look good. "Hey, 'girlfriend'!" she said cheerfully to Morgan.

Morgan smiled politely. "Hi, Nancy."

"Whaddya say? You ready to kick it?" Then Nancy's eyebrows drew together. "Honey, why do you still have pj's on?"

"It's been pretty busy," Morgan said, "around here."

Nancy walked into the apartment. "Wow! It's very neat," she said, surprised. "Did you guys get a maid?"

"No. Not exactly," Morgan answered.

At that moment, Giselle stepped out of the bathroom, followed by Robert.

"What is going on here?" Nancy cried, spotting the pair.

"Nancy!" Robert stared at her, stunned. He had completely forgotten that she was coming to pick up Morgan that morning! This was not good.

Fuming, Nancy pointed at Giselle. "Who is this?"

"Hello!" Giselle smiled sweetly, adjusting her towel. "I'm Giselle! I was on my way to the castle to get married and . . ."

Nancy wheeled on Robert. "She's married?"

"No!" he cried. "She's not! Not yet!"

Nancy narrowed her eyes. "What do you mean 'yet'?"

What *do* I mean? Robert wondered. He somehow felt that he had just answered the wrong question. He tried to get back on track. "Nancy! She was lost! I was helping her—"

"With what?" Nancy demanded.

"Nancy, calm down!" Robert begged. "Let's talk at least."

"Don't bet on it!" Nancy turned toward the door.

"But what about taking Morgan to school?"

Robert asked. "You know, some 'grown-up,' girl-bonding time?"

"What?" Nancy eyed Giselle with a sneer. "I don't think so!" Her BlackBerry chirped, but Nancy ignored it, storming out in a furious huff.

The door slammed behind her.

"Nancy, wait!" Robert cried, following her into the hall. He ran down the stairs and dashed into the street, but it was too late. Nancy's cab was already pulling away.

Well, Robert thought, as he watched Nancy's taxi turn a corner, that could have gone a lot better. Confused, and a bit annoyed, he took the elevator back up to his apartment. But when he tried to go into his bedroom, he found the door locked. He knocked impatiently.

"Hello?" Giselle answered brightly.

"Okay, you know what? You've got to go," Robert told her through the door. "Now! I don't know what your deal is. If you're waiting on Prince Charming or—"

"Prince Edward!" Giselle corrected.

"Whatever!" He heaved a heavy sigh. "I'll get you to a bus, a train, a plane, wherever! I can't get involved after that!"

Giselle walked out of the bedroom wearing a bright green peasant dress. Twirling about, she moved into the living room.

"Where'd you get that?" Robert asked.

"I made it!" She smiled at him. "Do you like it?"

Made it? Out of what? Robert's eyes drifted toward the living room window . . . where a dress pattern had been cut out of his curtains. He shook his head.

"You're unhappy?" Giselle asked.

"You made a dress out of my curtains," Robert pointed out.

"Oh, you *are* unhappy," Giselle cried. "I'm so sorry. I—"

"I'm not unhappy," Robert snapped. "I'm angry!"

Giselle blinked. "Angry?"

"Yes. It's an unpleasant emotion. Have you ever heard of it?"

Giselle thought hard. Anger. Yes, she had heard

of it. But she hadn't really believed it existed. It was like unicorns or fairies. Except that those things were real and anger, well . . .

"Look, you have created a completely unnecessary problem with Nancy that I now have to resolve," Robert shouted. "The fact is I was just getting ready to take a very serious step forward with her. A proposal, actually . . ."

Giselle gasped. A proposal! How romantic!

"But now," Robert went on, "she has it in her mind that you and I, well . . ."

Giselle's eyes went wide in horror. "Kissed?"

Robert nodded. "Something like that."

"Why don't you sing to her?" Giselle suggested. "Maybe that would reassure her of your affections!"

"Sing to her?" Robert looked doubtful. He wasn't really the singing type. Well, maybe "Happy Birthday," you know, if he really *had* to . . .

"You need to rush to her side and hold her in your arms and pour your heart out . . ." Suddenly, Giselle began to dance around the living room. When she realized that Robert was staring at her, she stopped in her tracks. "Why are you staring at me?"

"I don't know." Robert shrugged. "It's like you escaped from a greeting card or something."

"Is that a bad thing?"

Robert was about to say that he wasn't sure *what* it was, but then Morgan stepped out of her room, fully dressed and wearing her backpack.

Robert checked his watch—and the news was bad. "School! We're late. We've got to run!"

As he dashed into his room to get dressed, Morgan looked up at Giselle. "Don't worry," she whispered. "Daddy's a little cranky, but he's smart. I'm sure he'll help you get back to your prince."

Smiling, Giselle wrapped Morgan in a warm hug. She just hoped that the little girl was right.

Chapter Eight

Far away in Andalasia, Queen Narissa was working very hard to make sure Giselle did *not* get back to her prince. Staring into the magical wishing well, Narissa watched as the beautiful Giselle hugged the little girl. She clenched her fists tightly.

"Oh, wouldn't she just love to come crawling back here and steal my crown?" she sneered. "Cast me aside like so much royal rubbish." While Narissa would have been happy to continue her rant, her voice trailed off as leaves began to fall on her head and shoulders.

Angrily, she looked up only to see Nathaniel. He was standing on a ladder, clipping away at shrubbery to make a Narissa statue.

"Perhaps Prince Edward won't find her," he said hopefully.

Narissa nearly choked in anger. "Perhaps he *will!*" she screamed.

The scream was so loud—and scary—that it caused Nathaniel to jerk back. He wobbled on the ladder for a scary moment before steadying himself. Unfortunately, the Narissa statue's head was not so lucky. Nathaniel had snipped it clean off! With a gasp, he watched as it fell into the well and disappeared.

Watching the head fall, Narissa had an idea. Forcing a smile on her face, she turned back to Nathaniel.

"Oh, I do wish there was someone who cared enough for me to go after him," she cooed. "A man like that? I'd do *anything* for him."

That was all Nathaniel needed to hear. In one swift move (or rather, as swift a move as possible for

Nathaniel) he leaped off the ladder and into the well. He would make his queen happy . . . no matter what it took.

Back in Times Square, the manhole was revealing yet another arrival from Andalasia. With a loud cry and a thud, the recently replaced manhole cover blew off. This time, the sewer workers saw two plump legs sticking out, while the jettisoned cover spiraled like a top on the ground nearby.

Here we go again, Arty thought as he and his crew tugged at the plump waist-coated man in tights. Finally, they yanked him out of the hole and placed him upright.

The man stared, wide-eyed at the chaos of Times Square.

"You looking for a beautiful girl, too?" Arty asked.

"No," Nathaniel admitted, "I'm looking for a prince, actually."

Arty nodded. "Right."

Hey, at least this time I can point the guy in the right direction, Arty thought. Right up the street.

Following the man's finger, Nathaniel let out a gasp. It was the prince all right—and he appeared to be in trouble.

"You've met your match, foul bellowing beast!" Prince Edward was shouting at a crosstown bus. He and Pip were riding its roof as the vehicle turned onto Seventh Avenue. With a mighty stroke, the prince stabbed his sword through the roof of the bus.

Inside, commuters screamed and scrambled to avoid the blade. It pierced a bag of bird feed in an old lady's lap. Crumbs and seeds scattered every-where as the bus driver slammed on the brakes. She opened the doors and stood up, ready to give this kook some real New York attitude.

Just then, Edward leaned over and popped his head through the open doorway.

"Giselle?" he asked, looking around in vain. "My love? Drat!" Suddenly, he noticed the commuters. "The steel beast is dead, peasants!" Edward announced. "I set you all free!"

"Are you crazy?" the bus driver hollered. She stormed off the bus so that she could get a better look at the maniac on her roof. "Nobody stabs my bus! I'm gonna tear you apart! You hear me? You get down here right now!"

"Madam," said Nathaniel, who had caught up to the bus and now appeared at her elbow, "if you'll allow me . . ."

"Nathaniel," Edward cried happily, "old friend!"

The bus driver looked Nathaniel up and down. Yep—he definitely looked like a friend of the maniac on the roof. They obviously had the same tailor. "Crazy, tights-wearing . . . come here and mess up my route?"

At that moment, Pip dove lightly from the roof and onto the driver's head. Even though he couldn't speak, he balled up his little fist and shook it at Nathaniel. "I'll tear you both apart!" the bus driver went on, oblivious to the small animal on her head.

Nathaniel's eyes drifted up to Pip.

"Don't you roll your eyes at me!" the bus driver shouted. Suddenly, she realized that something was on her head. "Ahhh!" she screamed. "A rat!"

"Strictly speaking," Edward said from his perch

on top of the bus, "he's a chipmunk!"

"Get him off me!" The bus driver swatted frantically at Pip. He dodged her blows, racing around the small space at the top of her head. "Get it away! I hate 'em!"

As the driver screamed, sirens could be heard in the distance. Someone had called 911 to report the bus incident, and the police were on their way.

Nathaniel didn't know what the loud noises meant, but he knew that it couldn't be good. "Sire, perhaps we should search elsewhere for your bride?" he suggested.

"A sage thought, Nathaniel!" Prince Edward leaped from the top of the bus. "These peasants are quite ungrateful!"

Pip, who was quickly tiring of dodging blows, couldn't have agreed more. He hopped onto Edward's shoulder, and the three darted down a side street, leaving the furious bus driver behind.

Meanwhile, Robert was dealing with his own drama. After getting Morgan to school he headed to work. Unfortunately, Giselle had had to come along.

Now, Robert hurried out of the elevators with Giselle close behind. They walked into the elegant reception area of the law office where he worked. "Sam," he said to the receptionist, "please don't tell me Mrs. Banks is already here."

The young woman behind the counter looked deadly serious. "Mrs. Banks is already here."

Robert winced. "Oh, no!"

"Along with Mr. Banks and his lawyer," Sam went on.

"Perfect!" Robert's heart thundered in his chest. "How long have they been here?"

Sam arched an eyebrow. "Do you really want to know?"

Robert shook his head. "No, I don't. I need you to handle something for me, okay?" He leaned over Sam's desk, lowering his voice to a whisper. "This girl . . ." He gestured toward Giselle, who had just picked up an empty glass that was sitting on a side table.

"Who is she?" Sam asked.

"I have no idea," Robert admitted.

As they watched, Giselle walked over and dipped the glass into the office aquarium. Then she took a drink. Sam was trying hard not to stare, but given Giselle's unsettling behavior, that was quite impossible.

"I'm pretty sure she's from out of town," Robert admitted.

"Well, what did you want me to . . . ?"

"I don't know!" Robert cried. "Just . . . find out where she's from and get her there. And make it cheap. I'm probably going to end up paying for it. Oh, and if Nancy calls, let me know. I need to talk to her!"

Sam looked at Giselle again. "I bet." While the woman's green dress wasn't exactly modern, it *was* flattering against her red hair and pale skin. It occurred to Sam that she looked like a fairy-tale princess—a fact that would clearly *not* go over well with her boss's girlfriend.

Sighing, Robert approached Giselle. "Okay," Robert spoke slowly. "I have a critically important meeting here. Sam's going to help you get home."

"Mmm-hmm!" Giselle said agreeably. She couldn't really talk—her mouth was full.

"Stay out of trouble," Robert begged.

Giselle nodded brightly. She waited until Robert turned away to spit the tropical fish she had drank accidentally back into her glass.

Wow, Giselle thought as she looked at the pretty fish. The water here sure is *fresh!*

She was too busy admiring the fish in her glass to notice that a face had appeared in the tank behind her. Reflected in the shimmering water was Queen Narissa . . . who was scowling at Giselle with a look of pure fury. This was not good.

Meanwhile, Nathaniel, the prince, and Pip had entered a delicatessen to find something to eat. Placing an unconvincing chef's hat on his head, Nathaniel hurried through the busy restaurant kitchen lifting pot lids and then slamming them down again. He hadn't come here for just the food. He was desperately looking in every pan for Narissa!

"Nathaniel!" a familiar voice shouted from somewhere nearby, causing the portly man to jump rather ungracefully.

"My dearest queen! I'm here," Nathaniel cried out, searching in vain for his beloved. Lifting the lid on a nearby pot of soup, he gasped. Queen Narissa was staring right at him! "My goddess! My vision of loveliness!"

"Finally! I'm boiling in here," Narissa screamed. "Have you found her yet?"

Looking anxiously around the room, Nathaniel caught several of the chefs staring at him. Lowering his voice, he whispered into the pot, "I'm afraid I haven't, my lady."

Narissa rolled her eyes and impatiently gritted her teeth. "Time is of the essence," she seethed through the soup. Suddenly, three poison apples glugged up in the liquid, each oozing noxious vapors.

Nathaniel recoiled in horror. Nearby, one of the nosier chefs caught sight of the apples and turned away, repulsed by the smell. Using the pot lid as a shield, Nathaniel continued to talk with Narissa, his voice barely a whisper. "Poisoned apples, my lady?" A chill went down Nathaniel's spine. "Do you mean that you want me to . . . ?"

"Nathaniel," the Queen lowered her voice to a sultry whisper. "If there's ever going to be a 'happily ever after' for us . . . ?" She pouted slightly, her red lower lip glistening as she let the words sink in.

"Happily ever after!" he longingly repeated.

"It won't be difficult," Narissa went on, in a silky voice that could charm even the coldest of snakes, not to mention a lovesick page. "Just one bite. That's all it takes. One small bite to drag her down into a deep and troubled sleep! When the hands of the clock strike twelve?" She grinned, showing a row of gleaming white teeth. "That precious little pretender to my throne will be gone!"

Nathaniel's heart was beating furiously. He and his beloved . . . together? It was worth the sacrifice. He reached into the soup and grabbed the apples. "It shall be done, my lady! I promise!"

"You'll find her at Columbus Cir . . ." But before the queen could finish the word, a frantic waiter scooped up a ladleful of soup and with it, the queen's image.

As the now faceless liquid went completely still,

Nathaniel saw a new reflection on its surface. A chipmunk was looking down at him from a nearby rack. Pip had overheard everything! Now he knew just how much danger his Giselle was in. Nathaniel couldn't let him get away. He leaped at Pip.

But Pip was too fast. He jumped out of the way and scrambled back into the deli's dining room.

Prince Edward had just gotten his food when Pip darted onto the counter and slid onto his tray. Frantically, he tried to communicate to the prince what he had seen. Unfortunately, the prince was more handsome than he was clever.

"Pip?" Edward said in confusion.

"Sire, I beg you," Nathaniel panted as he hurried after the chipmunk, "don't listen to this insane little vermin. He's probably eaten some bad nuts or something!" He gritted his teeth. "Maybe we should put him down for his own good!"

"Nathaniel, please!" Prince Edward silenced the valet with a glance. "Let him talk!"

"But, sire . . ."

"Go ahead, Pip. What is it you want to say?"

Pip knew that getting Edward to understand him was going to be rather difficult. After all, the prince had little patience for anything that wasn't about him directly. And Pip was right. Despite his valiant efforts and rather clever pantomiming, Edward could not grasp what the chipmunk was trying to say.

"Nathaniel's glad to have me near?" Prince Edward guessed. "You feel you'd die without me here? You think me brave and cavalier?"

Pip balled up his fists. No, no, no! The prince had it all wrong! Why did he have to be so full of himself? Pip collapsed on the tray. Not being able to speak was so frustrating!

"All of that might be well and true, Pip," Edward said with a smug smile. "But we really have more important things to worry about right now."

Nathaniel heaved a big sigh of relief. Things were fine . . . for now. But he had to find a way to get rid of that meddlesome chipmunk.

Chapter
Nine

Nancy's BlackBerry buzzed for what seemed like the hundredth time that day. She looked at it but didn't pick it up.

"Robert again?" asked Nancy's assistant, May.

May was very fashionable—as fashionable as Nancy's high-ceilinged loft space that housed her fashion company. It was important to look chic when you were in the fashion business. Even the seamstresses busily stitching clothes on their sewing machines were dressed neatly. It was all part of the image.

Nancy glanced at the message on the BlackBerry. "Another text message apology."

"How many does that make?" May asked.

"I'm not sure, exactly," Nancy admitted. "I'm pretty sure not enough."

May tucked a pencil behind her ear. "So what are you saying? You're never going to forgive him?"

Nancy picked up a blouse from her new line, and began to inspect it very carefully. "I'm sure I will . . . at some point. I mean, it's not like I'm one of those women who sit around their entire lives waiting for some perfect prince in shining armor to take me off to his castle in the Hamptons. I got over that fantasy a long time ago!" She barked a laugh.

Oh, but it had been a *nice* fantasy—a prince on a white horse riding up the Hamptons' beach. . . . But who was she kidding? It just wasn't going to come true. Suddenly, Nancy ripped the shirt in half, surprising herself. Taking a deep breath, she handed it back to the confused seamstress. "With Robert and me, it's real, you know? I can count on him. At least, I thought I could."

May lifted her eyebrows. "You want to know what I think?"

Nancy rolled her eyes. "Is that a multiple-choice question?"

"I think you're a hopeless romantic who's discovered romance is hopeless," May told her boss.

Nancy had no comment. "You can't find anything else to do?" she demanded.

Back at Robert's office, his very-important meeting had just come to an end. "Well, I think that went well," Robert said as he escorted Phoebe Banks to the reception area. Phoebe's eyes were slightly sad, but otherwise she seemed in control. Her soon-to-be ex-husband, Ethan, was right behind her, followed by his lawyer. "You know, there's no reason not to be reasonable."

Ethan Banks's lawyer, Henry, nodded in approval. "I think we might actually be in the neighborhood of a settlement."

Just then, Robert noticed that Sam was waving frantically in his direction. "Will you excuse me? I'm going to check on your cars," Robert said. He walked over to Sam's desk. "What? What is it?"

Sam nodded toward Giselle. "She has no driver's license!" she hissed. "No passport. I can't even find this place she's talking about!"

"What place?" Robert asked.

"Andalasia? I've called every travel agent!" Sam waved impatiently at her computer monitor. "Every airline! I don't know if it's a country, a city . . ."

". . . a state?" Robert suggested weakly. He looked over at Giselle, who was grinning dreamily. She was dancing around in circles to the easy-listening music piped in over the office sound system. Robert gulped. Honestly, this was his biggest fear—that Giselle was completely, one hundred percent *bananas*. She certainly looked it right now, twirling about like a pinwheel.

Sam was watching her, too. "More like a *state of mind*," she said. "She told me it's just beyond the 'Meadows of Joy' and the 'Valley of Contentment.'" She cast a nervous glance around the room before whispering, "I mean, what's that all about?"

Giselle stopped twirling. "Oh, my goodness!" she cried, catching sight of Phoebe. "You're beautiful!"

"Oh!" Phoebe blinked in surprise. No one had called her beautiful in a long time. "Well, thank you!"

"The man who holds your heart is a lucky fellow indeed." Giselle sighed.

Phoebe cast a glance at Ethan, who was chatting with his lawyer. "Try telling *him* that," she grumbled.

"Oh, I'm sure he already knows!" Giselle chirped.

"Excuse me?" Realizing that he was being talked about, Ethan turned to face Giselle and his almost ex-wife.

"Oh, are you him?" Giselle asked with a huge smile. "You must be so happy! The way her eyes sparkle! No wonder you're in love!"

Ethan gaped at Giselle. "Is this a joke?"

What is she doing? Robert thought as he watched the scene in horror. For a moment, he was too stunned to move.

"I would never joke about love," Giselle said honestly. She took hold of each of their hands. "You make such a handsome couple."

Phoebe and Ethan looked at each other, then quickly glanced away. Phoebe pulled her hand from Giselle's.

"Giselle—please!" Robert hissed, hurrying over to separate Giselle from the Bankses. "It's not like that, all right?" He tried to keep his voice down. "They're not together anymore."

Giselle blinked her blue eyes blankly. "I don't understand."

"They're getting a divorce," Robert explained. And when Giselle still didn't understand, he added, "They're separating from one another."

"Separating?" There was a tremble in Giselle's voice. "For how long?"

"Forever," Robert said.

"You mean forever and *ever?*" Hot tears sprang up in Giselle's eyes. They spilled onto her cheeks. She felt weak and dizzy. Forever and ever! It was the worst thing she had ever, ever, *ever* heard!

"Are you crying?" Ethan stared at her, then turned to Robert. "Is she actually crying?"

Giselle simply couldn't stand up anymore. She sank into a little puddle on the floor, sniffling miserably.

"I'm sorry," she said between her sobs. "I can't help it. That's so sad!"

Phoebe pressed her lips together. Giselle looked how she felt—brokenhearted. Phoebe had been doing her best to seem calm and cool ever since the moment Ethan had told her that he wanted a divorce. But there was something about seeing Giselle so miserable that was making her feel as if she was about to cry. Well, she wasn't going to cry. Not in front of Ethan, that was for sure. Instead, she got angry.

"What kind of place are you running here?" Phoebe asked Robert. "This is so *unprofessional!*" She stalked over to the elevator quickly, so that no one would see the tears in her eyes.

"Phoebe," Robert called, "wait!"

The elevator doors opened. "Good morning, Phoebe," Robert's boss, Carl Churchill, said as he stepped out of the elevator. "How are you . . . ?"

But Phoebe pushed past him, and the elevator doors closed behind her.

Henry than wheeled on Robert. "If you guys are

trying to manipulate us," he snarled, "you can throw this whole deal out." Then he, too, stormed out of the office, with Ethan close behind.

Carl frowned at Robert. "What was that all about?" He looked at Giselle, who was still crumpled on the floor in a tearful heap. "Who's she?"

"She's a friend," Robert stammered, "an acquaintance. I . . ."

"Robert," Carl said sternly, "you're the one who begged me to put you on a case, and this is what I get? I walk in and find everybody upset. What is going on here?"

"I'll take care of it," Robert said quickly. "Carl, it's gonna be fine."

Carl didn't say "good," or "I'm glad to hear it," or "I trust you, Robert." He didn't say anything at all. But his silence told Robert what he needed to know—he'd *better* take care of it. Or else. He tugged Giselle up by the arm, pulling her away from the reception area. "What is wrong with you?"

"Me?" Giselle was surprised. Why would Robert think there was something wrong with *her*? She was not the one about to be separated from her true love forever. Or, at least she hoped she wasn't.

"Yes, you. This whole routine of yours?" Robert demanded. "Those people are in real pain!"

"Well, no wonder they're in pain!" Giselle cried. "Separated forever? Married one day and the next day they're not? What kind of awful place is this?"

The elevator doors opened, and Robert hurried Giselle inside. "It's called 'reality'!" he cried, pushing the button for the lobby.

"I think I'd rather be in Andalasia."

Robert snorted. "I think I'd prefer that, too! Get in please."

"I wonder if we might cover more ground separately, sire" Nathaniel said, as he, Edward, and Pip entered into the area of New York known as Columbus Circle. "You by yourself and me with . . ." He sneered at Pip. ". . . it?"

"An inspired plan, Nathaniel!" Edward cried.

But Pip had just noticed something—Giselle! She was across the street, with a man Pip didn't know.

Pip let out a squeak. Edward didn't notice, but Nathaniel did. Looking over, he spotted Giselle, too. Quickly, he grabbed Pip in a firm fist, silencing him.

Edward looked around. "Where do you suppose I should look . . . ?"

"Look, sire!" Nathaniel shouted, pointing over the prince's shoulder, at a young woman who was most definitely *not* Giselle. "Do you see her? Over there!"

"Giselle?" Edward cried. "Where?"

"Hurry!" Nathaniel cried, shoving Edward away from where he could spot Giselle. "Run to her! Not a moment to lose!"

Edward darted off in the wrong direction.

And Nathaniel, still holding Pip, started after Giselle.

Chapter Ten

"I tried to do the right thing here," Robert said as he pulled Giselle into Central Park. "To be nice . . ."

"You've been very nice!" Giselle said.

"And I've been severely punished for it! I can't help you anymore, Giselle!" Robert exclaimed loudly. His anger faded as he handed her a few bills. "Look, here's some money. Just . . . take it! Call up your prince. Have him pick you up, bring his horse, whatever, because I honestly just can't handle it!"

Giselle stared in confusion at the money in her hand. "Robert?"

"Just go!" Robert begged. "Please!"

"I'm so sorry, Robert," Giselle said softly. For the first time, she really looked at him—as a person. And she had to admit, he looked miserable. Suddenly, she was overcome with a rather awful sensation. She felt terrible! She had never meant to make him so sad. "You've been a kind friend to me when I had none. I'd never want to make you unhappy or cause you trouble. So I'll go now. I wish you every happiness." Forcing herself to give him one last smile, she turned and walked away.

Robert did not move for a moment. Finally, he turned and started to walk back to his office. I did the best I could, he thought. I couldn't have done anything else. And sure, she is beautiful, but she is one odd duck. He glanced over his shoulder at Giselle . . . and let out a gasp.

Giselle had already stopped . . . to talk to an old homeless woman. And now she was handing over the money Robert had given her!

Robert rolled his eyes in frustration. What is she *doing*? he thought as he trotted back to

Giselle. She can't be left alone for a minute.

"Oh, it was him," the old woman was saying as Robert ran up. "I'm sure of it!"

"Do you really think so?" Giselle asked eagerly.

"Giselle," Robert interrupted, "what are you doing?"

"Robert!" Giselle grinned hugely. "This is Clara. She says she saw Edward!"

"He was on a bus this morning!" Clara nodded, wagging her finger. "He tried to kill me!"

"Really?" But Robert wasn't really listening. He had taken Giselle by the arm and was now trying to steer her away from Clara. "That's great. Thank you." He lowered his voice to a whisper. "What are you thinking?" he asked Giselle. "You can't just *give* people money."

"You gave me money," Giselle pointed out. "Besides, she was so very helpful about Edward!"

Robert sighed. Of course she would say something like that. "What's the deal with this 'prince' of yours, anyway?" Robert asked. "How long have you two been together?"

"Oh, about a day," Giselle replied matter-of-factly.

"You mean it feels like a day?" Robert steered Giselle onto one of Central Park's footpaths. "Because you're so in love?"

"No," Giselle corrected. "It's been a day."

Robert's eyes went wide. "You're kidding me. A day? One day? You're joking."

"I'm not," Giselle said.

"Yes, you are."

"But I'm not."

"You're getting married to someone after *one day?*" Robert couldn't believe his ears. "Because you fell 'in love' with him?"

"Yes."

Robert shook his head in amazement. This was so very like Giselle—unbelievable and fantastical. The woman was going to drive him batty! Didn't she know that love didn't happen in a day? This was all too much. He couldn't digest this information—not on an empty stomach, at least.

Oh, what the heck, Robert thought. It's almost lunchtime, anyway. Walking to a nearby vendor, he bought himself and Giselle hot dogs. "I don't get this," Robert said as Giselle tore happily into her lunch. "How can you talk about loving some guy you don't even know?"

"I know what's in his heart." Giselle took another bite.

"Oh. Right. Of course." Robert huffed.

"Mmmmm-hmmmm!" Giselle's mouth was stuffed with hot dog—she had to chew and swallow before she could speak. "It's so yummy! I never knew food could taste like this!" Robert took her now empty wrapper and tossed it in the trash. "And what about you? How long have you known your Nancy?"

"Five years," Robert said.

"And you haven't proposed? No wonder she's angry!" Giselle found herself quite impressed with Nancy's patience. She never could have waited five years to marry Edward! Twenty-four hours was bad enough!

"*Hel*lo, nice lady," said a strange voice, breaking into her reverie. It was a food vendor, dressed in a white apron and cap. But it was not really a vendor.

It was Nathaniel. He was speaking in a very bad Russian accent and holding out a delicious-looking caramel apple. "You want juicy sweet caramel apple, maybe? No charge for the beautiful young woman."

"Free?" Robert looked at the apple suspiciously. People rarely gave out anything for free in New York.

"Of course," Nathaniel said with a big, fake grin. "Today is free caramel-apple day. Tomorrow is free beef jerky!"

Suddenly, his grin disappeared. A captured Pip was trying to escape from Nathaniel's pants! The chipmunk wiggled and squirmed inside his back pocket, making it rather uncomfortable for Nathaniel. Finally, Pip darted free and leaped at the apple. Nathaniel caught him before Giselle noticed he was there.

"Well, thank you, kind sir!" Giselle said. The apple certainly did look wonderful.

"Quite welcome . . . *misssssss!*" Nathaniel hissed as Pip bit down on his hand. Nathaniel popped the chipmunk into a popcorn maker.

"You know that apple's pure poison, don't you?"

Robert asked as she was about to take a huge bite.

Giselle looked startled.

"All the preservatives in that caramel could kill you," he explained.

She lowered the apple, giving it a suspicious glance.

"It's a joke," Robert said quickly. "I'm just saying," he went on as he and Giselle walked away from Nathaniel, "normal people spend time getting to know each other before they get married. They date."

Giselle cocked her head. "Date?"

"Yeah, you know? A date!" Robert said. But it was clear that Giselle didn't know what he was talking about. "You go someplace special," he explained. "You know, like a restaurant. Or a movie, museum. Or you just hang out and you talk."

Giselle thought for a moment. "What do you talk about?" she asked. This whole "date" idea sounded fun.

"About each other," Robert said. "About yourself. About your interests. Your likes. Your dislikes. You talk."

Giselle couldn't help laughing a little. "You have such strange ideas about love!"

"Oh. Maybe I should do it your way," Robert teased. "Meet. Have lunch. Get married . . ."

"You forgot about 'happily ever after,'" Giselle prompted.

"Forget about 'happily ever after'!" Robert cried. "It doesn't exist!"

Giselle was horrified. "Of course it does!" she cried, waving her hands wildly. Her wild gestures caused the apple she was still holding to slip from her grasp. It arced into the air, landing on a passing man's bicycle helmet. It stuck there as he and the pack of cyclists he was with sped off.

"Giselle, I hate to disagree with you," Robert went on, unaware that her apple had disappeared and was now being pedaled far, far away. "But most marriages are considered a success if they manage to *not* end, period. Forget about happiness."

"How can anybody forget about happiness?" Giselle wanted to know.

Robert thought about that. Sadly, he had more

experience in that area than he cared to admit. "It happens."

"But you and Nancy?" Giselle prompted. "You know you will live happily ever after, right?"

"Look, I don't know if we'll make it through today, let alone a whole lifetime," Robert pointed out. "That's what I'm trying to tell you, Giselle. It's complicated."

"Oh, but it's not!" Giselle insisted. "Not as long as Nancy knows how much you really love her!"

"Yeah . . . well . . . of course she knows." Robert nodded his head, as if he was certain she knew. "I mean, we don't talk about it every single minute of the day, but she knows. . . ."

"How?" Giselle demanded.

"What do you mean, 'how'?" Robert asked. He was beginning to grow impatient.

Giselle stopped in her tracks. Did Robert not tell and show Nancy how much he cared? How could this be? Overwhelmed by the thought, Giselle broke into a song about the importance of letting people know how you feel about them.

"What are you doing?" Robert asked when she began to sing.

Giselle did not answer. Instead, she continued to sing her way through the park. Soon, all different sorts of people were singing and dancing. It looked like one, big party! There was a steel drum band, a traveling troupe of actors—even a Polish dance group—and they were *all* singing!

"Would you just stop," Robert begged. "Please?" He actually felt like he might die of embarrassment, right there in the middle of Central Park. New Yorkers did *not* do cheery sing-alongs in public!

But there was no stopping Giselle! Then, all around her, while people sang and danced, Giselle gathered up a bouquet of beautiful wildflowers. Not satisfied, she added a few special blooms from the displays created by the city of New York. Giselle whistled a happy trill, and two doves flew down to meet her. "Could you take these to Nancy, please?" she asked the doves in a normal voice.

"Are you crazy?" Robert demanded. "They don't **know where she is! They're birds! Hey,"** Robert said as the doves flew away with the bouquet, "how'd you get them to . . . ?"

But Giselle was already off, dancing and singing with a group of in-line skaters.

When the song *finally* came to an end, Robert looked up to find himself surrounded by a park full of new friends: kids, businesspeople, joggers, Polish dancers, steel drummers, cyclists—even a few guests from a Japanese wedding. All of these people had joined in Giselle's song. In spite of himself, Robert found the whole scene . . . enchanting.

His BlackBerry rang with a chirp. Robert clicked it on.

"Robert?" Nancy's voice was breathless. "I love the flowers!"

Robert's mouth fell open in shock. She actually got the flowers? He stared at Giselle.

Maybe she wasn't as crazy as he thought. And maybe there was something to this love business, after all.

Robert hurried over to Nancy's studio. Since he

didn't know what to do with Giselle, she came along. And—as he was quickly growing accustomed to—Giselle immediately found something to gush over. She actually enjoyed the studio very much. The sewing machines were fascinating!

As soon as Nancy got over the fact that Robert had brought Giselle along, she smiled. She pulled Robert into a private corner. "I just love them so much!" she gushed, looking over at the flower arrangement. The doves were nestled among the flowers, cooing.

"Really?" Robert was delighted.

"Yeah, usually you send those e-mail cards with the digital flowers. These are exquisite. Where do you find live doves in New York City?" Nancy cried. "And these?" she added, holding up a pair of golden tickets. "We're going to a ball?"

Robert winced. How had those gotten in there? He would have to speak to Giselle later. "We don't have to. I just thought . . ."

"Are you kidding me?" Nancy squealed. "This is so romantic! So spontaneous! I can't wait!"

"Good," he said. "Well . . . that's good. Listen, as far as Giselle. I was only helping her. Honestly, I . . ."

Before he could go on, Nancy held up a hand. "If you say nothing happened, then nothing happened. I trust you."

Robert smiled. Well, that was easy, he thought. "So, tomorrow night, then?"

"This is so unlike you!" Nancy said, giving Robert a hug.

He smiled over at Giselle, who was busy twirling about in a bolt of white fabric. He never would have guessed that someone could be so good at getting him into trouble . . . *and* at getting him out of it.

Chapter
Eleven

"It appears this odd little box controls the magic mirror!" Prince Edward said as he carefully aimed the remote control at the television set.

After chasing the wrong woman all afternoon, Edward had declared he was tired. So he, Nathaniel, and Pip had reunited and found a room in a seedy hotel. Unfortunately, Pip was being held prisoner in a popcorn box. Nathaniel had convinced the prince that the chipmunk needed his rest.

At the moment, Edward was reclining on the bed, fascinated with the "magic mirror." He flipped the channels, past sports, a commercial, a Spanish-language show, and finally landed on the local news. A reporter was interviewing the bus driver that Edward and Nathaniel had met—rather unfortunately—that morning. "There was these two guys dressed all freaky, and then this chipmunk shows up all crazy and biting!"

Edward nodded. The mirror seemed to know of their adventures. He changed the channel again, landing on a soap opera.

A beautiful woman gingerly treated a bruise beneath the eye of a handsome man. "I only hit him because I'm in love with you!" the man said.

"You think I'll love you just because you go out and bully everybody?" the woman asked. "You think it makes you strong, but you're weak and sniveling and pathetic!"

This was of no interest to Edward. He pressed the button on the remote.

"Wait, sire!" Nathaniel cried as the channel changed. "Go back!"

Fumbling with the remote, Edward managed to flip back to the soap opera.

"How could I ever love a man who doesn't even like himself?" the beautiful woman was now asking.

Nathaniel stared at the magic mirror, amazed by the television's wisdom.

Meanwhile, Pip had managed to punch his way out of the popcorn box. Quickly, he leaped from the table onto Edward's stomach. Then, he tried to act out Nathaniel's evil plans to poison Giselle.

"Nathaniel likes the way I leap?" Edward asked Pip, once again assuming everything had to do with him. "I'm handsome even when I sleep?"

"Sad little chipmunk!" Nathaniel said as he scooped up Pip and carried him toward the closet. "Deranged from exhaustion. Maybe you'd like to snuggle in a nice little nook for the night!" He hung Pip on a clothes hanger, between two metal clips, and shut the door. "I think I need some air, my lord. . . ."

"Very well, Nathaniel." Prince Edward kept his eyes on the television.

Nathaniel opened the door to leave. "Sire?" he asked, stopping suddenly. "Do you like yourself?"

After being tricked by the evil
Queen Narissa, Giselle finds herself
in the middle of Manhattan!

Prince Edward has arrived from Andalasia in search of his one true love, Giselle.

Robert is a serious lawyer who doesn't believe in fairy tales.

At Robert's apartment, Giselle shows off her new dress, made from his own curtains.

Edward and his "loyal" companion, Nathaniel, are lost and looking for Giselle in Manhattan.

Edward dreams of the day
he can return
to Andalasia with his love.

Giselle helps Morgan make
breakfast for her dad, Robert.

Giselle and her prince
head out on a date.

Queen Narissa will stop at nothing to keep Giselle from the throne.

Will Robert give Giselle the
kiss of true love in time?

Giselle, Robert, and Morgan have
found their "happily ever after."

Looking up, the prince gave Nathaniel a self-satisfied smile. "What's not to like?"

Nathaniel thought about that for a moment. Then he turned to go.

But inside the closet, Pip hadn't given up. Faster and faster he swung himself on the hanger—right over the rod and down onto the floor. He was still wearing the hanger, but that didn't bother the chipmunk. Scurrying past the bed, he hopped onto the window ledge. Using the hanger, Pip managed to force the window open. The hanger snapped off, and he scrambled after Nathaniel.

Pip had to stop him!

Meanwhile, in a different part of the city, Giselle let out a giggle. Robert had taken her to an Italian restaurant. She was sitting at a table with a warm pizza in the middle. And in a very uncharacteristic move, Robert was entertaining Giselle—with magic. Well, a magic trick at least.

"Oh, do it again!" she squealed in delight when he pulled a coin from behind her ear. A moment later,

Giselle's eyebrows furrowed, and her expression grew thoughtful.

Noticing the look, Robert asked, "What?"

"This is a very nice place," she answered slowly.

"Yeah," Robert responded.

"And we're eating together," she continued. Then her eyes grew wide as she announced, "This is a date!"

For a moment, Robert was speechless. Why would Giselle say that? Was she right? She couldn't be! This was not part of the plan. Quickly, he explained. "No, no, no, no! We're just . . . we're just . . . friends!"

At the word friends, Giselle smiled in relief. That was good. After all, Robert wasn't her true love. Edward was.

"Besides," Robert added, "people don't usually bring their kids on dates."

Giselle nodded and looked across the restaurant.

Morgan was sitting at a corner table, helping the woman who owned the restaurant fold napkins.

"She's a wonderful girl," Giselle told Robert as

they both watched Morgan. "So sweet and kind and gentle."

"Yeah," Robert agreed. "She's great."

Giselle frowned.

"What?" Robert asked.

"Does she miss her terribly?" Giselle asked, her eyes on her plate.

"Miss who?" Robert asked.

"Her mother."

"Oh . . . well . . . we don't usually talk about that," Robert said with a shrug.

"Was it very sad?" Giselle's voice was gentle. She was afraid that she might not like the answer.

"It didn't start out that way," Robert said. He smiled, but it was a sad smile. "But love, that lovey-dovey version you like to talk about, that's a fantasy. And eventually you wake up in the real world." He sighed. "She left me."

That *was* a sad story, Giselle thought. "I'm so sorry for you both."

"Thanks. I'm a big boy." Robert nodded toward Morgan. "It's her I worry about. She's really shy, she doesn't have many friends, and I just, I want her to be strong, you know? To be able to face life for what it is. That's why I try not to encourage all this fairy-tale stuff, setting her up to believe all this unrealistic 'dream come true' nonsense."

"But dreams do come true!" Giselle insisted. "Maybe something wonderful could happen."

Robert looked at Giselle's face—beautiful and bright with hope. "I forgot who I was talking to."

"I hope you don't forget!" She smiled shyly. "I like talking to you."

For a moment, Robert and Giselle just sat quietly, looking deep into each other's eyes. It felt as if everything and everyone had just faded away. Giselle's breath caught in her throat. Her heart began to beat faster.

"*For-a the nice lady!*" boomed a voice.

The spell was broken. Robert and Giselle looked up to see a waiter standing before them, holding a bright green drink. They didn't realize that the waiter was Nathaniel, who had tracked them down, again. Or that the drink was poisoned! "*From-a secret admirer.*"

"Secret admirer?" Robert glanced around the restaurant. "Why is everyone always giving you free stuff?"

Giselle peered at the drink, unconcerned by details. "Oh, really? What is it?"

"*Eets an apple-a marteeni, Mees!*" Nathaniel said in a horrible, fake Italian accent. Sure enough, there was a slice of red apple in the drink.

"Pretty," Giselle said. "It looks yummy."

"Careful," Robert warned. "Those things are deadly! They have a way of sneaking up on you."

"I'll just have one sip," Giselle said.

"*A sippa ess all it a-takes!*" Nathaniel crowed.

But just as Giselle lifted the drink to her lips, a chipmunk appeared from beneath the checkered tablecloth and knocked the glass from her hand.

Robert jumped backward. "What in the—"

"No!" Nathaniel bellowed as the glass crashed onto the floor.

"Pip!" Giselle cried, thrilled to see her old friend.

"You miserable little . . ." Nathaniel stepped back,

realizing that he couldn't throttle Pip here—Giselle would realize who he was.

"What is it, Pip?" Giselle asked as the chipmunk started trying to act out the danger that she was in.

"Hey, can we get some help here?" Robert hollered, as the other customers in the restaurant began to notice that there was a *creature* on the table.

Pip struck a heroic pose.

"Edward?" Giselle squealed, understanding her furry friend perfectly. "Here?"

"We've got a rodent at our table!" Robert called.

Now the people in the restaurant gasped.

"That's wonderful!" Giselle clapped her hands together.

"A chipmunk!" Morgan shouted, hurrying over to get a closer look.

"Don't touch it, Morgan!" Robert pushed her behind him. "They're loaded with diseases!"

"I'm going to be a princess!" Giselle said dreamily. She gave Pip a kiss on the forehead. Thrilled, Pip leaped onto her shoulder and began showering her in kisses.

"It's chewing off her face!" screamed an elderly woman, misinterpreting the gesture.

"That rat's attacking her!" shouted a gentleman near the back.

"Help her!" begged a young mother. "Someone!"

"*I'll save-a you, miss!*" Nathaniel shouted as he took a broom and swung it at Pip.

"Leave him alone!" Giselle cried, but Nathaniel swung again.

Pip leaped into the air as Robert pulled Giselle away from the table. The chipmunk landed back on the table. He hid beneath the pizza, as if it were a blanket.

Nathaniel growled in frustration. He had lost Pip . . . again! Then he noticed that the pizza was moving. "*There you are-a, you menace!*" Grabbing the pizza, he flung it across the room. The pizza and the platter it was on spun like a Frisbee—straight into the pizza oven. Immediately, a small black cloud of smoke poured out.

The customers burst into applause.

Nathaniel blinked in surprise. All of these people were clapping for *him*.

Giselle burst into tears. Robert, misinterpreting her tears for relief, put one arm around her and the other around Morgan.

But Giselle was not relieved. She was distraught. She had no way of knowing that Pip hadn't been on the pizza when it went into the oven. He had fallen off, right into a carafe of wine. He was a little dazed, but he was okay.

It didn't take long for the television news to show up at the restaurant. Of course, the reporter wanted to interview Nathaniel right away. "People are calling you a hero!" she said.

"*Well-a*," Nathaniel said with a blush, "*you do what you-a gotta do!*"

"Well, I think you're amazing!" the pretty reporter gushed. She beamed up at Nathaniel.

He was so surprised by the positive attention that he forgot to use his accent. "Really?" he said. A hero. No one had ever called him that before. It felt good.

Chapter
Twelve

"Tell me, magic mirror," Edward said, looking straight at the television, "what is this awful place? Why is everything so . . . difficult? Will I *ever* find my heart's duet?"

He changed the channel, and a news bulletin appeared. And on the mirror was—Giselle! "A preliminary search of the pizza oven did not reveal any rodent remains," the reporter said. "This animal's still out there somewhere! Also with us is the woman who was actually attacked by this insane chipmunk!" The reporter turned to Giselle. "How does it make you feel, knowing this dangerous animal is most likely still alive?" She held out the microphone.

"It's wonderful!" Giselle glowed, thrilled at the happy news. "Pip is the most amazing friend I've ever . . ."

"Giselle," Robert said, appearing at her elbow, "why don't we go home? C'mon."

"Good-bye!" Giselle called to the reporter. "Lovely to meet you!"

"Giselle!" Prince Edward cried, leaping toward the television. "What villainy is this?"

"Is this unprovoked attack part of a new trend?" the reporter asked, looking into the camera. "Is urban-rodent rage on the rise? Only time will tell. . . ."

Edward drew his sword. "Magic mirror, I beg you! Tell me where Giselle is!"

"Reporting from one hundred sixteenth and Broadway," said the reporter on the screen, "I'm Mary Ilene Caselotti."

"One hundred sixteenth and Broadway!" Edward exclaimed. He knelt before the television to give it a huge hug. "Thank you, mirror!"

Later that night, Giselle tucked Morgan into bed. "Were you scared back there?" Giselle asked gently as Morgan pulled the covers up to her chin.

"A little," Morgan admitted. "Do you think Pip will be okay?"

"Oh, I wouldn't worry about Pip." At least, not now that we know he didn't land in an oven, Giselle thought. "He's very brave. I remember one time that poor wolf was being chased by Little Red Riding Hood in her grandmother's house! And she had an axe! If Pip hadn't been walking past to help . . ."

"I don't remember that version." Morgan said softly.

Giselle pursed her lips. "That's because Red tells it a little differently!" She didn't want to say anything against Red, but that girl could tell some serious whoppers.

Standing in Morgan's doorway, listening to Giselle's tales about Pip and Red, Robert found himself smiling. He had to admit, Giselle told wonderful stories.

"Good night, Giselle!" Morgan said, snuggling against her pillow. "Thanks for the story."

"You're welcome, dear," Giselle said with a smile. "Sweet dreams." She closed Morgan's door carefully, leaving only a slight crack for light to get in. Moving into the living room, she plopped onto the couch— her bed. But she wasn't ready to sleep. A book was resting on the coffee table. Giselle picked it up. *Important Women of Our Time*, the cover read. Giselle flipped through it, hoping to find something about princesses and prince charmings.

What Giselle didn't know was that *her* prince charming was closer than she could have guessed.

Prince Edward had followed the advice of his magic mirror and found the restaurant where he last saw his love. Making use of his abilities as a hunter, he sought out signs of Giselle and soon found himself in front of Robert's apartment building.

Once inside the building, Edward faced a new challenge: struggling to make sense of this seemingly infinite hallway of identical doors. He took a brave step forward and knocked on one's surface, and then instinctively jumped back. He quickly struck an action pose, his sword poised high as he prepared to gallantly sweep in and save his damsel in distress.

When the door opened, he was surprised to find not Giselle but a tired-looking woman—a tiny, wailing baby in her arms—and three more children shrieking as they raced about the apartment behind her. The woman looked at Edward with a combination of disdain and hopelessness. Then, with a grunt, she slammed the door in a very confused Edward's face.

And so the night went on. He tried again and again, moving down the line of identical doors, knocking on each and quickly striking his pose in anticipation of finally finding his bride-to-be. But after a while, and many slammed doors, his boundless enthusiasm began to wane.

In another part of the building, as Edward's mission was just getting started, Robert was walking out of the bathroom, his hair still wet from a shower. Catching sight of Giselle on the couch, he cleared his throat. "Listen, Giselle. That was a nice story. About your chipmunk friend and all, but . . ."

Giselle looked up from her book. "Um . . . yes?"

"I know what it's like when someone disappoints you. It's tempting to want to see things how you wish they were, instead of how they are."

"I don't wish that he's coming, Robert," Giselle said. "He is."

"Right." Robert heaved a heavy sigh. "Because the chipmunk told you . . ."

"That's right. Pip said that actually he—"

Robert interrupted her. "You know what? I don't know if you're being funny or ironic, but chipmunks can't talk."

Giselle thought that over. She had to admit that Robert *might* have a point. "Not here they don't."

"So in lieu of taking advice from a forest rodent . . ." Robert said in a gentle voice, ". . . I just wanted to say . . . if it did turn out you decided to stay in New York, I could help you. If you needed to talk to an immigration lawyer, or get a job, find a place. I'd like to help. . . ."

Giselle's eyebrows drew together in a confused frown. "That's very kind, Robert, but Edward is coming for me."

Robert forced himself to stay calm. He didn't want to get upset with Giselle, but he was starting to feel very frustrated at her refusal to face facts and at her rather annoying devotion to this Edward. If he really did love her, wouldn't he be here with her now, instead of him? Trying to keep his voice level, he said, "Yeah, but if he doesn't . . ."

"Why do you keep saying that?" Giselle snapped.

"Because!" Robert threw up his hands. "I deal with this stuff every day! Usually when a relationship has issues at the beginning, things don't get much better!"

"He is coming!"

"Giselle, I don't think so. No—"

Giselle stood up. "Yes!" she shouted.

"I'd have to disagree. No!"

"Is that the only word you know?" Giselle cried, her face turning red with fury. "'No'?"

"No!" Robert winced. That didn't come out the way he meant it too. "I . . . I mean . . . no."

"No! No! No!" Giselle hollered, clenching her fists. "Over and over again! Every word out of your mouth is no!" She stormed across the room. "Robert, sometimes you just make me so . . ."

Robert cocked his head. "Make you so . . . what?"

Giselle stopped in her tracks. Slowly, she turned to face him. "Angry!" she said. There was amazement in her voice. "I think I'm angry!"

"Really?" Robert's eyebrows flew up. "Are you okay?"

"Yes. I feel . . ." Giselle took a deep, ragged breath. Being angry had set her whole body on fire! "Wonderful . . ."

"You sure?" Robert touched her shoulder gently. He was a little concerned.

"Oh, yes." Giselle swallowed. She had never been this close to Robert before. He smelled wonderful. "I'm fine!" she said quickly. "Fit as a fiddle!"

Robert looked at her carefully. "Okay," he said slowly. "Good night." He walked toward his room, and Giselle flopped back down on the couch.

This world is full of so many strange, wonderful

things, Giselle thought. And awful things, too. And then there were things that were wonderful and awful at the same time. It was all so very confusing. No wonder Robert was so hard to understand!

The next morning, Robert woke up a little later than usual. Peering into Morgan's room, he saw that her flowered curtains had dress-shaped cutouts in the centers. "Oh, no!" Robert groaned, realizing that Giselle was already awake—and making herself busy around the apartment.

"Morning, Daddy!" Morgan chirped as she helped Giselle set the table.

"Good morning, Robert," Giselle said, her cheeks pink and her hair gleaming in the morning light. Robert had to admit she looked very pretty in her new curtain dress.

Forcing his eyes from Giselle, Robert scanned the table. It was set with delicious-looking food. There were eggs, strips of crisp bacon, pancakes—all of Robert's favorites. "Breakfast!" he said happily. "Great."

Then, the doorbell rang.

"I'll get it!" Morgan shouted, running to answer the door.

Robert and Giselle looked at each other, unsure what to say. Their argument the night before had left them feeling awkward. "Nice dress," Robert said finally. She had made herself a little apron, too.

Giselle blushed. "Thank you."

"It is I!" shouted a voice in the hall. "Prince Edward of Andalasia! I've come to rescue my lovely bride, the fair Giselle!"

Robert's jaw dropped. "Oh, my . . ."

"He's here!" Giselle whipped off the apron she was wearing. "Oh, my! Oh, my goodness! How do I look?"

"Slightly stunned?" Robert said.

Giselle rolled her eyes impatiently. "I meant, how do I *look?*"

"You look . . ." Robert paused, searching for the right word, ". . . beautiful."

Before she could respond, Morgan led Edward into the living room. "Giselle!" he cried, beaming at her. He had never felt happier. There was nothing Edward liked more than a successful quest. Unless it was killing trolls, of course.

"Edward!" Giselle smiled, and before she could say another word, Edward lifted her into the air. He twirled her around, accidentally knocking a small vase and a china animal from the coffee table.

"No problem," Robert said quickly, picking up the knickknacks and placing them back on the table. "Nothing broken."

Edward ignored him, giving Giselle another twirl and knocking everything over again.

"Could you please be careful?" Robert asked, bending over to pick up his things.

"You!" Edward shouted, his gaze finally settling on the other man in the room. Edward put down Giselle and drew his sword. "You're the one who's been holding my Giselle captive?" He pointed the sword at Robert. "Do you have any last words before I dispatch you?"

Robert gave him a dubious look. "You've got to be kidding me!"

"Strange words," Edward said.

"No, it's all right, Edward," Giselle said, moving to stand in front of Robert. She took Morgan's hand in hers. "These are my friends," she explained.

"Oh." Edward put his sword back in its sheath and cleared his throat. He gazed at Giselle, starry-eyed. Then he began to sing—loudly. But when Giselle did not return his gaze or his song, he looked at her, confused. Was she not happy to see him?

Giselle noticed his confused look and held out her hands apologetically. "I'm sorry. I was just thinking."

"Thinking?" Edward was surprised. Thinking was something he did very little of in Andalasia. It never seemed to lead to anything good.

"Before we leave," Giselle said nervously, "there was just one thing I was hoping to do. It's a strange exotic custom they partake of here."

Edward bowed deeply. "Name it, my love, and it is done!"

"I want to go on a date," Giselle said.

Edward cocked his head at the strange word. "A date?"

"Um . . . yes." Giselle glanced at Robert. "Well . . . we go out to dinner and we talk, about ourselves. Our likes and our dislikes. Our interests." She gave Edward a nervous smile. "A date!"

A date. Prince Edward thought it over. Frankly, he was a little disappointed. He'd rather hoped that Giselle would ask him to slay something—a dragon or monster or some such. But he didn't see any reason not to go on a date. Perhaps during this date event, they would happen upon a dragon. And he didn't mind talking—as long as it was about him.

A short while later, Morgan and Robert walked down to the street with Giselle and her prince. Giselle was surprised by the emotion flooding through her. She had expected to be elated by Edward's arrival, but instead she was sad. She wasn't ready to say good-bye.

And it appeared Robert and Morgan weren't all that ready to say good-bye yet either. The four stood awkwardly for a moment before Giselle broke the silence.

"You know you can come visit Andalasia anytime . . ."

Robert nodded, trying to remain positive. "And if you ever come to town we should all get together for dinner."

"Yes, that would be lovely," she smiled hopefully. But her words sounded hollow to her ears as she realized that neither of them really believed it would happen. There was another long pause as they both struggled to think of something else to say to make the moment less painful.

"We'll all see each other soon," he finally said, unconvincingly. "It's not like we're talking about, you know, forever. . . ." His voice trailed off.

". . . and ever," she finished for him softly.

Robert could feel her eyes searching his face, but he couldn't bring himself to look at her directly. "So, uh . . . good luck on your date."

Giselle felt a strange pang to hear him say this, but she tried to smile and reply in kind. "And you with Nancy." He nodded and shifted uncomfortably.

Giselle turned to Morgan. "It's been so nice

spending time with you, Morgan. I—"

Morgan threw her arms around Giselle's neck, wrapping her in a tight hug. Giselle hugged back, fighting the tears that sprang into her eyes.

Soon—much, much too soon—Edward tapped Giselle on the shoulder. She wanted to stay there, hugging Morgan forever, but she knew she couldn't. Straightening up, she gave Morgan and Robert a final wave.

Edward eyed Robert. "Thank you for taking care of my bride, peasants!" he cried, leading Giselle away.

Morgan looked up at her dad. "I'm going to *really* miss her," she said sadly.

"Me, too, sweetheart," he replied, trying to sound stronger than he felt. "Me, too."

Chapter
Thirteen

"I don't know how they found each other, My Queen!" Nathaniel cried miserably. "I really don't." He was sitting at a table in the Italian restaurant, looking down into his drink while waiters bustled around him.

"You idiot!" Narissa growled, looking up from the water in his glass.

"But Your Majesty?" Nathaniel blinked at her.

"I sent you to kill her, not save her!" Narissa shouted. "Can't you get that straight?!"

"I realize you're upset, madame," Nathaniel said.

"But if you can find your way to give me one more chance . . ."

"Another chance?" the queen demanded. "You think poison apples grow on trees? There's only one left! You're out of chances!"

"But Your Majesty!" Nathaniel cried again.

"Forget it!" Narissa screamed. "I'm coming there . . . I'll kill that little wretch myself!"

Ka-boom! Nathaniel's glass exploded—along with every other glass and bottle in the restaurant. Narissa's scream had shattered them! A wine carafe cracked, and a very surprised chipmunk tumbled out. Pip landed right in front of Nathaniel.

Looking up, Pip gulped. He was in trouble all over again.

Meanwhile, Robert was having a strange meeting at his office. He was sitting across from Ethan and Phoebe Banks . . . who were holding hands and staring into each other's eyes.

"I was thinking about what that girl said," Ethan gushed, giving his wife's hand a squeeze. "About

Phoebe's eyes sparkling. You know, that's the first thing I noticed when we met. I mean, look at her! It's true! They really do sparkle!"

Phoebe blushed. "Ethan . . ."

Robert shook his head as the Bankses gave each other a light kiss. This is beyond weird, he thought. "Look," he said, "I have to say, as your attorney, Phoebe, you shouldn't let a chance encounter . . ."

"Maybe it wasn't chance," Phoebe said. "Maybe it was no accident we met her."

"I'm sorry." Robert looked doubtful. "I find that very hard to believe."

"Maybe you need to try harder," Ethan suggested.

"Look, you guys had problems!" Exasperated, Robert ran his hands through his hair.

"Everyone has problems!" Phoebe shot back. "Everyone has bad times. Do we sacrifice all of the good times because of it?"

Robert opened his mouth to reply . . . but he couldn't think of anything to say. "You're not making me feel like a very good divorce attorney," he admitted.

Phoebe smiled at him. "Maybe you're not," she said.

"Did you like your hot dog?" Giselle asked as she and Edward walked over a bridge toward Brooklyn. Their date had lasted nearly all day. They had seen the Statue of Liberty, the Empire State Building, and the Central Park Zoo. Edward was even wearing a green foam crown shaped like Lady Liberty's and carrying a handful of balloons. He was exhausted. This date had been more tiring than searching for Giselle in the first place.

Edward stared at his lunch. "Dog?"

"It's not really made of dog," Giselle said quickly. "It's just what they call it here. A hot dog."

"Quite excellent," Prince Edward pronounced, attempting to stuff the last bit of bun into his mouth in a regal manner. He chewed, swallowed, and then said, "Well, that was a splendid date. Shall we go?"

"Where?" Giselle asked.

"Back to Andalasia, of course!" Edward said,

extending his arm. "To be married and live together happily ever after forever and ever."

"Well, we don't have to go right away. . . ."

"How long do these dates usually last?" Edward asked, rather impatiently. Theirs had already been going on for more than five hours.

"As long as you want them to," Giselle said brightly. "They can just keep going and going, if you keep thinking of things to do. There's all sorts of activities. . . . We could go to a museum! Or to the theater. There's even this ball—"

Edward smiled. "A ball?" That, at least, was something he had heard of.

"You'd like that?" Giselle asked. "Dancing? Music?"

"Well," Edward hesitated. He really wanted to go home and get married. "I suppose, but . . ."

"Wonderful!" Giselle cried, clapping her hands. "We have to go!"

"And then home to Andalasia?" Edward asked hopefully.

"Of course!" Giselle forced herself to smile. "The moment it's over!" She squeezed Edward's hands happily. "Oh, I have so much to do to get ready! I have to figure out what to wear . . . my hair."

"And what shall I do?" Edward asked.

Giselle stood back to look at him. His princely clothes were worn and dirty, and the prince himself was smelling a bit . . . ripe. "There's something really magical here I think you should probably try."

"What is it?"

Giselle smiled warmly. "A *shower*."

Morgan stood in front of the mirror, wearing a princess gown. It had always made her happy to wear it before. But now it just reminded her of Giselle.

Suddenly, Morgan noticed something strange in the corner of her mirror. It looked almost like . . . "Giselle!" she cried, running to give her friend a hug. "You're back!"

Giselle knelt down to look Morgan in the eye. "I need your help!" she said desperately. "I'm going to the ball, and I'm not sure what to do or what I should wear, and I don't even know where to find a fairy godmother at this late hour!"

"I have something better than a fairy godmother!" Morgan said, taking Giselle by the hand. Morgan led Giselle into Robert's bedroom. She pulled a gold credit card out of his sock drawer. "Daddy says it's only for emergencies," Morgan whispered. "This is definitely an emergency!"

Morgan's babysitter had fallen asleep in front of the television, so she and Giselle tiptoed out of the apartment.

All we have to do is get back before she wakes up, Morgan thought as they hurried off. I'll deal with the fallout later.

Right now, they had some shopping to do.

Chapter Fourteen

Three hours later, they had it all: dress, bag, shoes, hair accessories, lingerie, makeup, jewelry, perfume. Now Giselle was seated in front of a mirror at a salon. Her wet hair was wrapped in a towel, while beside her, Morgan was getting her toenails done and giving her some last-minute advice. "... and when you go out, you don't want to wear too much makeup," the little girl said.

Giselle flashed her a grateful smile. "You know, I couldn't have done this without you. You were such a big help."

Morgan beamed. "Really? Thanks."

"You're welcome," Giselle said.

Morgan looked down at the magazine in her lap. After a moment, she looked up at Giselle. "So is this what it's like?" she whispered.

"What, sweetie?"

"Going shopping with your mother?" Morgan asked.

Giselle thought for a long moment. "I don't know," she finally admitted. "I never went shopping with my mother."

"Me, either." Morgan couldn't keep the sadness out of her voice completely.

"But I like it," Giselle added. She smiled at Morgan, and Morgan smiled back.

"Me, too."

"Just think," Giselle said, giving Morgan an encouraging hug. "Soon you'll have a new mother."

"You mean *step*mother," Morgan corrected.

"That's not true, what they say," Giselle said. "I've known so many kind, wonderful stepmothers. You know, Edward's got a stepmother. I've never met her, but I hear she's just lovely."

Morgan sighed. Nancy was okay, but she wasn't sure how she felt about having her for a stepmother. No matter what Giselle said.

Back in the middle of Times Square, a man sat in the driver's seat of a taxicab listening intently to the radio. It was Nathaniel in his latest disguise—cab-driver. But at the moment he wasn't driving, he was too engrossed in a radio talk show.

"Mister N is on the line telling us his sweetie pie is acting a little 'distant.' You were saying, Mister N?" The host grew silent as someone began to speak. It was Nathaniel! He had found a cell phone and called into the show.

"I've always treated her like a queen," he said into the cell phone, "but lately, I'm starting to feel there's this whole other side to her, like I don't even know her anymore."

The radio call-in host was used to hearing about difficult relationships. But even she thought that this "Mister N" person had a scary woman on his hands! "I think you need to take her aside and ask her, what's the deal with this relationship?"

"Maybe you're right." Nathaniel nodded. "Maybe I need to do that."

"Exactly." The host of the radio show brightened. "Find out how she really feels about you."

"Hello, worthless!" growled a voice.

Looking up, Nathaniel saw the beautiful, yet cruel, face of Queen Narissa through the passenger window. She had arrived in New York City—and she did *not* appear happy. He hung up quickly.

Perhaps now wasn't a great time to talk about their relationship.

Moments later, Queen Narissa looked into the misty waters of a nearby fountain. Her black cape waved in the evening wind, and her purple shadowed eyes were as cold as ice. Nearby, Nathaniel stood with Pip in his arms. He had locked the chipmunk in a round hamster ball after finding him at the restaurant.

"*Reperio lemma mihi!*" the queen shouted, gazing into the water. The image in the fountain was dim, but it grew brighter. . . .

"You know," Nathaniel said suddenly, "lately I feel you've treated me with unwarranted hostility. And I'm just wondering if maybe we need to talk . . . maybe reevaluate where our relationship is headed."

The queen glared at him, then turned back to the fountain, not bothering to answer. "*Reperio lemma mihi!*" she exclaimed instead, raising her arms.

Slowly, an image of Giselle and a fresh-looking Prince Edward appeared in the mist. They were in the lobby of the Woolworth Building, heading toward the elevators.

Narissa smiled cruelly. This time, she thought, Giselle is *mine*.

Nancy and Robert swept across the ballroom floor to the sound of lively music. The ballroom had been decorated to look like a palace, and everyone was dressed as if they were in a fairy tale. Nancy looked beautiful. She wore a romantic old-fashioned ball gown that was something a princess might wear, and her dark hair had been curled into tight ringlets. Atop the curls was a sparkling tiara. But despite the outfit it was hard for Nancy to feel like a princess. Robert had been distracted all evening, and she couldn't help wondering what was wrong. "What are you thinking about?" she asked.

"Everything, I guess," Robert admitted. He tried to make himself sound cheerful. "You and me. The future."

"Really?" Nancy batted her eyelashes at him. "And what does this future look like?" The music ended, and Nancy dropped a curtsy. But Robert wasn't watching. Or breathing. His eyes were fixed on the top of the staircase—where Giselle had just appeared. "What is she doing here?" Nancy asked following Robert's gaze and watching as Edward removed Giselle's cape.

Unlike the other partygoers, Giselle wore a sleek, sophisticated modern dress and, of course, a pair of glass slippers. Her red hair had been straightened and fell long past her creamy shoulders. She looked absolutely beautiful.

"I have no idea," Robert answered absently.

Standing at the top of the stairs, Giselle took in

the ball. For the first time since Giselle had arrived in this world, everyone else looked like they belonged in Andalasia, and she looked like she belonged here! It was a rather odd sensation. Taking a deep breath, she and Edward started down the staircase . . . where Robert was waiting.

"I'm a little surprised to see you," Robert said.

"I'm surprised, too." Giselle smiled shyly. "You told me you couldn't dance."

"I said I *didn't*," Robert corrected. "I never said I couldn't."

From his place beside her, Edward cleared his throat.

"Oh, excuse me!" Giselle said, turning to Nancy. "This is Edward. He's my . . . prince."

"And this is Nancy," Robert said to Edward. "She's my . . ." But he wasn't sure how to end that sentence.

"We're together," Nancy explained, hugging him.

"And this beautiful lady is Giselle," Edward said gallantly. "The love of my life, my intended, my heart's true desire!"

Nancy's eyes widened. "Wow."

"Is something wrong?" Edward asked.

Nancy shook her head, impressed. "Just the way you said that," she said. "So straightforward and unself-conscious. Not a hint of irony. It's very . . . romantic." She smiled.

"Well, thank you." Edward gave her a small bow as the bandleader stepped to the microphone.

"Well, folks," the bandleader said. "It's the time of the night we look forward to all year long. So in keeping with tradition, I'd like to ask each gentleman to turn to a lady he did not accompany this evening and invite her to dance the King and Queen's Waltz." The band struck up a slow tune.

Edward bowed toward Nancy. "May I have the pleasure?" he asked.

Nancy glanced at Robert, who nodded. In a moment, she and Edward danced away.

Robert offered Giselle his arm. "Shall we?"

She gave him a small curtsy.

As they danced into the middle of the room, Giselle looked into Robert's eyes and felt her heart flutter.

Robert leaned toward Giselle's ear. Softly, he sang along with the bandleader, and Giselle felt herself relax into his arms, her head against his shoulder.

Above, clouds of golden confetti fell down from the ceiling. It was like magic. . . .

"Mind if I cut in?" asked a voice behind Giselle. Nancy was standing there, nodding at Robert.

The moment was shattered. Giselle stepped back. "No!" she said. "Of course."

Nancy stepped into Robert's arms.

Tears welled up in Giselle's eyes, making Nancy and Robert look blurry as they twirled away.

Edward took her hand, leading her up the stairs. "You're sad?" he asked.

Giselle made herself smile at him. "Oh, no, I'm fine!" She had never told a lie before, but she just didn't know how to tell him the truth. She wasn't even sure what the truth was. That she loved Robert? How was that even possible? They were from different worlds!

"I'll get your wrap," Edward said.

Giselle leaned against a pillar as the band played

on. It really was time to go home.

Looking down, Giselle watched as Nancy leaned in to kiss Robert. Giselle felt as if her heart had been torn in two. True love's kiss, she thought. The most powerful force on Earth . . .

"Hello, my dear!" said a creaky voice behind her.

Wheeling around, Giselle saw a dark, hunched shape. She gasped. It was the old hag! She was truly hideous, with wrinkled skin and cruel eyes. "You? What are you doing here? You're the one who—"

"I'm so glad to see you, child," said the hag. "I've been so very worried! Such a terrible accident, your coming to this place." Her eyes glittered like hard stones as she peered at the dancers below. "With so much sadness. So much pain. Oh, yes. To never be with the one you love, doomed to be with another . . . For eternity. Oh, but it doesn't have to be like that. Oh, no, no, I can stop the pain, make all those bad memories disappear." Slowly, the old hag reached into her robe and pulled out a glossy red apple. "One bite, my love, and all this will go away. Your time here, the people you've met. You won't remember anything. Just sweet dreams and happy endings. But you must hurry! The magic won't work unless you take a bite before the clock strikes twelve."

Giselle cast another glance at Robert. He was still dancing with Nancy, holding her close. Then she looked at the apple. Don't I want to forget? Giselle thought. Isn't it easier for everyone that way? She lifted the apple to her lips.

The old hag smiled as a giant thunderbolt crashed overhead, rattling the building.

Giselle fell to the floor in a heap as the red apple— one bite missing—rolled from her fingers.

Chapter
Fifteen

Meanwhile, in a cab outside the Woolworth Building, Nathaniel was once again lamenting his romantic situation. Only this time, his listener was not a talk show host, but rather, Pip, who was still trapped inside the plastic hamster ball.

"She talks about us having a future," Nathaniel complained, "but all she really cares about is this nasty apple business!" Nathaniel continued to pour out his frustrations while Pip listened. Not that the chipmunk had a choice. After all, he *was* locked inside a hamster ball. "And I'm helping her!"

Nathaniel went on. "I mean, what does that say about me?"

From inside his hamster wheel, Pip acted out what he thought it said about Nathaniel . . . and it wasn't pretty.

"No, you're right." Nathaniel shook his head grimly. "You're absolutely right. . . ." Suddenly, he made a decision. He reached for the door handle but stopped to turn back to Pip. "Thanks for being a great listener," he said gratefully.

Pip sighed. He didn't want to be a good listener. He just wanted to help Giselle!

Back in the ballroom, the old hag—a limp Giselle in her arms—was shoving her way through the crowd toward a waiting elevator. "Out of my way!" she snarled. Once inside, she placed Giselle on the floor and then whispered a few magic words, "*Speciosus, formosus, praeclarus* . . ." As the elevator doors slowly closed, the old hag's face began to shift and change. In moments, she had grown younger and very beautiful—she was Queen Narissa!

But suddenly, the elevator doors stopped moving. A sword had been wedged between them, forcing them open. In a moment, the queen was face-to-face with the prince.

"Edward?" Narissa fumbled.

"Mother?" His eyes were wide with shock.

Narissa tried to hide her surprise. She glanced at Giselle's limp body, then at her stepson's angry face, then back at Giselle. "Oh, my . . . I was taking her out for a little fresh air. She seems to have swooned."

But Edward wasn't listening. Pushing the doors open further, he rushed over to Giselle and knelt at her feet. "Someone help me!" he shouted, as he lifted her in his arms and carried her out of the elevator. "Please!"

"You're overreacting," Narissa said, following him. "She's fine, darling. Just give her some water. You needn't get so upset dear, really."

Below, the crowd was slowly becoming aware that something was happening above them—including Robert. Looking up, he saw Giselle unconscious in Edward's arms. Before he could think, he headed toward the stairs. Nancy followed a few confused steps behind. "Call 9-1-1!" he shouted to Nancy.

Meanwhile, Edward had placed Giselle down gently on a cushioned bench and was kneeling next to her. As soon as Robert arrived at the top of the stairs he rushed over and knelt beside him.

A bewildered Nancy pulled out her BlackBerry and dialed. "Hello? We have a woman here. She's unconscious. I didn't see what happened."

"Oh, well!" Queen Narissa sounded indignant. "She fainted."

"No, she didn't!" said a voice. It was Nathaniel. He was standing in the elevator, breathless.

The queen's eyes flashed dangerously. "Nathaniel?"

"You poisoned her!" Nathaniel cried, pointing at Narissa. "She's the evil hag! She poisoned her! With my help, I regret to say."

"You did this?" Edward sneered at the queen. Rage poured through him. He had never been more furious!

"He's lying!" Narissa insisted. "Why would I ever align myself with that buffoon?" The queen sneered at Nathaniel.

"You lying wretch!" Edward shouted at the queen. "When we return home, all of Andalasia shall know of your treachery! Your days as queen will be over!"

Narissa scoffed at his threat. "Take my crown? Don't you think that's a bit melodramatic, dear?"

But Edward had made his decision. "I will see to it that you will be removed from the throne *forever!*" he declared.

At the mention of forever, Narissa's face filled with fury! She would not let go of that throne! Raising her hand, she began to mutter, *"Latereo vox iam procer . . ."* But that was all she got out. The touch of steel against her neck silenced Narissa.

Nathaniel had leaped into action! "That's enough from you!"

Meanwhile, Nancy was still on the phone with the 911 operator. She looked down at Robert, who was still by Giselle's side. "They want to know what happened."

Robert looked at the apple. Nathaniel had been right. "She's been poisoned!" he shouted.

"We've got to help her!" Edward felt icy fear flood his veins. "What can we do?"

"I don't know." Robert felt sick. "I . . ."

From his spot by Narissa, Nathaniel spoke up, his voice sad. "There's no way of helping her now."

Dong!

The first stroke of twelve sounded, counting down the final moments before midnight. Narissa's face changed at the sound. She let out a wicked laugh. "He'll never save her now!" she cried. "When the clock strikes twelve, she'll be dead!"

Dong! Another chime sounded. And Narissa's evil smile grew wider.

Dong!

Dong!

Looking down at Giselle's beautiful face, Robert felt his heart break. Another chime sounded. This couldn't be the end. It just couldn't. Suddenly, he remembered Giselle's words. "True love's kiss," he said slowly. "It's the most powerful thing in the world. . . ."

"Yes. Yes, of course!" Edward stepped toward Giselle. "I knew that!"

Narissa's eyes grew wide. This was not part of the plan! They grew even wider as, leaning down, the prince kissed Giselle with all the love he could.

Dong!

Everyone waited . . . but Giselle didn't move.

Edward tried again.

Still, nothing happened.

Dong!

"It's not working!" Edward cried.

"She's done for now!" Nathaniel cried, while Narissa began to cackle maniacally.

Dong!

Edward stared at Giselle. She was dying. His kiss hadn't saved her. . . . How could that be? She was *his* true love! It was *he*—perfect and handsome Edward—who was supposed to wake her. But then why did she continue to sleep? Suddenly, a thought struck him, and the light dimmed in his eyes. He knew now what had to happen. "Unless . . ."

"Unless what?" Robert asked.

Edward looked up at him, his intentions clear even though not a word was spoken.

Dong! The clock chimed again.

Robert understood Edward's gaze immediately. "It's not possible!" he insisted. "It couldn't be me!"

"Don't you see?" Edward said gently.

Confusion flooded Robert's heart. "I barely know her. I've only known her for a few days. . . ."

Dong!

"Kiss her, Robert!" Nancy cried.

Robert turned to her, surprised that she would echo Edward's thoughts.

"You deserve true love," she said urgently. "We all do."

Dong! The eleventh stroke . . .

Robert gazed down at the sleeping Giselle. She looked so beautiful. In that moment he realized, without a shadow of a doubt, that she was his true love. That the racing heart wasn't nerves, but pure adoration. Slowly, he leaned forward.

"Please don't leave me," he whispered desperately. Then he pressed his lips against Giselle's and kissed her softly. It was a kiss full of hope and love. He leaned back and waited anxiously.

And . . . nothing happened.

Dong!

Narissa grinned. Too late! It was too late!

But just then, Giselle's cheeks turned pink. Her eyes fluttered open, and she looked up into Robert's face, her eyes filled with emotion. "I knew it was you," she said softly.

Around them, the crowd burst into applause.

But not everyone was happy. "Nooooo!" Narissa's screech echoed through the hall. With incredible strength, the queen twisted out of Nathaniel's grasp. Grabbing the sword, she began backing down the stairs. "The most powerful thing in the world . . ." she hissed, "I don't think so."

"You selfish, evil . . ." Nathaniel snarled.

But the queen was not to be threatened. "*Speciosus*," she murmured, "*formosus, praeclarus!*" A thunderous explosion knocked Edward, Nathaniel, and the guests around them backward. Edward's head cracked against a post, and he fell to the floor, unconscious. Nathaniel sprawled, limp, across a dinner table.

As the guests watched, Narissa stretched and grew, twisting and writhing. Green smoke clouded around her. When it slowly parted, it revealed a scaly body, talons, and a slithering tail. The beautiful queen had become a ferocious beast!

"All this nauseating talk of true love's kiss . . . it really does bring out the worst in me!" She let out a ferocious cackle. "You know, I've been thinking," Narissa continued when the transformation was complete. "What if a giant vicious beast showed up and *killed* everyone!" She took a menacing step toward Giselle, nostrils flaring. "Let's begin with the one who started it all, shall we?"

Robert stepped in front of Giselle. "Over my dead body!" he shouted.

The beast lowered her head and studied Robert carefully. Then, with a sneer, she said, "All right, I'm flexible." And scooping him into one of her claws, turned to Giselle. "Come along! You won't want to miss *this* ending!"

Then, as Robert twisted in her claw, the Narissa beast stomped across the ballroom, sending guests scurrying in every direction. She smashed through the giant windows, disappearing into the night.

And, while partygoers screamed and ran *away* from the ball, Pip was going *toward* the ball— though still inside his hamster ball. Despite the cage, he fought the wave of people coming at him to get into the elevator.

Back by the elevators, Nancy knelt down next to Edward, but he was out cold. Giselle stared at the ballroom. What about happily ever after? she thought desperately. But it was clear that she hadn't reached that part yet. She had no choice—she had to do something, or her chance at happiness would be gone forever. She hurried down the stairs, nearly tripping over Edward's sword.

Gingerly, she picked it up. Giselle tested its weight. Then, kicking off her glass slippers, she dashed out the window and after Robert.

Outside, Giselle picked her way along the outer balcony. The Narissa beast was holding Robert with her tail, dangling him over fifty stories above New

York City traffic. "What are you doing?" Robert cried. "Are you crazy?"

"No," the beast said. "Spiteful. Vindictive. Never crazy. Ow!"

Turning around, the Narissa beast's eyes grew wide. Giselle had just struck her tail with the sword!

"Well?" the beast said, her eyes glittering. "Our brave little princess comes to the rescue?" She turned to Robert with a sneer. "I guess that makes *you* the damsel in distress."

Turning from Robert, Narissa looked at Giselle. "Keep up with me, dear! It's time we take this tale to new heights." The beast let out a cruel laugh, then with a mighty leap, she jumped to the top of the building. Giselle climbed after them.

The beast held Robert in a claw, dangling him close to Giselle. She was daring her to follow.

"Go back, Giselle!" Robert begged. "It's too dangerous!"

"He's right, you know!" the beast taunted. "Playing the 'hero' can be quite dangerous. You might chip a nail!" The beast's tail cracked like a whip. Giselle rolled away just in time. "Or get a run in your stockings!" The tail snapped again, and Giselle dodged it again. Gritting her teeth, she climbed toward the top of the building after the beast.

While the Narissa beast howled in triumph from the top spire, below, Nancy, and a now conscious Edward and Nathaniel, made their way onto the outside balcony. Just then, Pip's hamster ball knocked against Edward's feet.

Edward looked down. Inside the ball, Pip was gesturing frantically. For the first time, Edward felt certain that he understood what the creature was trying to say. "You'd like to finally be released?" he said. "To help Giselle best the beast? Why didn't you say so in the first place?" Edward let the chipmunk out. In a flash, Pip scurried up the building's side.

"I'm not going to let you take him away!" Giselle cried as she tried to pull herself up onto the thin spire.

"I'm sorry," the beast said as she held Robert high overhead. "We're coming to the end of our tale now!" The Narissa beast cracked her tail once more, causing Giselle to lose her grip and tumble onto a lower ledge. Looking around, a familiar figure caught her eye.

"Pip?" For there was the chipmunk, as if he had been waiting for her. Pip gave her the thumbs up and climbed over Giselle. He scrambled up the spire. It was starting to bend under the weight of the beast. Suddenly, Pip had an idea! He had been in a similar situation not too long ago! He jumped onto the beast's head, pounding his fists into her skull. Thank goodness I didn't lose that weight! Pip thought as the spire bent further.

Gritting her teeth, Giselle pointed her sword at the beast. The spire bent still further, and the beast struggled to keep her balance. But she was starting to slip!

At that moment, Giselle hurled the sword with all her might.

It didn't hit the beast. The sword sailed past,

pinning Robert's sleeve to the spire. Just then, the Narissa beast lost its balance and tumbled down the side of the building.

Thump!

The beast landed on a turret. But it wasn't the beast anymore. The shock of the fall had caused the queen to turn back into herself. Pip, who had been clinging to the beast as she fell, now leaped from her head onto the safety of the balcony.

Narissa tried to hold on to the turret. But her hand slipped. Suddenly, she lost her grip, and with a shriek she plunged to the pavement below.

But Giselle was too busy to notice. "Hold on, Robert!" she cried as his sleeve began to rip.

He grabbed onto the spire, but his fingers began to give way. Four were left holding the spire, then three, then two. "Ahhh!" Robert cried as he fell . . .

. . . right into Giselle's arms. She pulled him backward onto the ledge. "Is this a habit of yours?" Giselle teased. "Falling off stuff?"

Robert gazed up at her. There was no doubt in his

mind . . . or in his heart. She was his true love. "Only when you're around to catch me," he said.

And then, for the second time—but not the last—Robert and Giselle shared true love's kiss.

Chapter
Sixteen

Back inside the ballroom, Nancy wandered aimlessly. The guests had left, and the musicians were packing up their instruments. Looking down, she spotted one of Giselle's glass shoes. The other had disappeared in the chaos. Nancy thought about her high hopes for the ball. Things hadn't turned out quite the way she had wanted. . . . Hot tears welled in her eyes, and she sank to the floor.

"Why so sad, beautiful lady?"

Prince Edward was standing over her. He held out a white handkerchief, which Nancy gratefully accepted.

"I think Giselle forgot her shoe," she said, holding up the slipper. She laughed sadly. "Figures."

Without a word, Edward removed one of Nancy's shoes. In its place, he put the glass slipper. "It's a perfect fit," he said with a smile.

Nancy gazed at the shoe, then up at Edward. She caught her breath. He's so romantic, she thought. So handsome . . .

Prince Edward was having similar thoughts. Nancy is brave and beautiful, he thought. And I can see that her heart is kind. Perhaps *she* is meant to be my princess. Looking deep into her eyes, Edward saw love flash, and he had his answer.

Grabbing her hand, they raced out of the ball-room and through the city on foot. Edward led her to the manhole, and the two of them leaped into Andalasia—together.

Epilogue

The very next day, at the palace in the magical world of Andalasia, Prince Edward and Nancy were married. It was a royal ceremony, and everyone remarked that Nancy made a beautiful princess. Edward became a good king and enjoyed many happy days troll hunting and governing the people. Nancy became known as Queen Nancy the Kind, for she spent her days helping the peasants, especially the children.

Nathaniel found a new career as a self-help author. He wrote a book titled, *My Royal Pain:*

Vanquishing the Evil Queen Within. It became a best seller, and Nathaniel helped thousands of unhappy men find the strength to like themselves.

Pip also found fame back in Andalasia, where he was finally getting the respect he deserved. Animals from all over the forest lined up for Pip to sign the autobiography he wrote about his adventures in New York City titled, *Silence Isn't Golden.* His book turned out to be a perfect cautionary tale to all the extroverted furry sidekicks out there, warning them to stay away from magical wells and evil hags.

And as for Giselle and Robert? Their life was just as enchanting. They were married and stayed in New York City. Giselle took over Nancy's old studio, renaming it Andalasia Fashions, where she made princess dresses for children. Morgan, meanwhile, was a flower girl in the wedding. And even better? She now got to go shopping with her new mother whenever she wanted.

So, in the end, everyone got their true heart's desire. And, of course, they *all* lived "happily ever after."